CLOCKWORK GIRL

Athena Villaverde

Eraserhead Press
Portland, OR

ERASERHEAD PRESS
205 NE BRYANT
PORTLAND, OR 97211

WWW.ERASERHEADPRESS.COM

ISBN: 1-62105-000-9

I lovingly dedicate this collection to the following people who were direct inspiration for its contents:

Rose O'Keefe, Carlton Mellick III, Zoe Welch, Robert Smith, Margery Williams, Francesca Lia Block, the members of Gotan Project and my fourteen-year-old self.

CONTENTS

CATERPILLAR GIRL

ONE

Something was wrong with Cat Filigree. Ever since her seventeenth birthday her skin felt tight, like someone had dipped her in glue. It slowly hardened and peeled off. Her feet felt too big for her body. Her vision was intermittently blurry and her sense of smell went haywire. Constantly feverish; she was burning up and freezing cold simultaneously. Her body itched. Her skin blistered and peeled off in layers. She was undergoing chrysalis.

Her mother, who had butterfly wings like stained glass windows, told Cat that soon it would pass. Soon all the loose skin on her back would form into her own beautiful set of wings and she would discover what type of butterfly she would be. But for now, she was still Cat, the caterpillar girl. High school student. Outcast.

Cat's high school was filled with the typical assortment of insect kids. There were the praying mantises who met after school in the courtyard every day. A tough Christian youth group; dedicated hardcore to praying and saving their country. They loved getting into sparring matches to show off for the lady bug girls how tough and pious they were.

The lady bug girls were the rich preppy girls that liked only the trendiest clothes and popular music. They all had the same style of perfectly coifed hair, light red skin with just the faintest smattering of freckles. They always kept their nails perfectly manicured and their antennas bent at the cutest and most stylish angles.

Then there was Larry, the stoner slug. Every day, he sat like a Buddha under the Bodhi tree in one of the few patches of shade in the desert schoolyard sorting through his Magic: The Gathering cards and eating Cheetos through his dreadlocks. Sometimes Cat ate lunch with him.

Other days, Cat ate lunch with Paulette, the moth girl. Paulette had naturally white hair and her waifish body and big eyes made her look just like the cartoons she drew. Everyone knew that Paulette would grow up to be a famous cartoonist. She had an ongoing strip in the school newspaper about a colony of bees in outer space. She and Cat liked to talk about comic books.

But Cat's favorite person, her best friend, was Lilith, the spider girl. All the boys were in love with Lilith—the preps, the jocks, the nerds and even the gay boys.

Lilith had long, slender black-and-white striped legs, a perfect ass, a tiny waist and high round breasts. No matter what she wore, she'd look amazing, but she always had the coolest styles. She altered all of her clothes herself, accenting them with punk rock embroidery and safety pins or cinching the seams on the sides of her shirts so they were more form-fitting.

She was the only spider girl at their school. There was a stigma against female spiders because after they had sex they would usually eat their mates. Lilith definitely had been known to do that.

When boys disappeared, people didn't talk about it much but all the girls hated her for it. They thought she was a dirty whore. Bad news.

Even though the boys knew that Lilith was dangerous, they still managed to get involved with her. Some of them probably even liked her because she was dangerous. Lilith called herself a nymphomaniac. She couldn't help it, she said, she just liked sex.

Lilith especially liked sex with butterfly boys, with their slender bodies and large colorful wings. They were usually musicians and artists. They would sneak her back stage at punk shows and buy her beer even though she didn't have a fake ID. Sometimes she would let them paint her portrait naked or sing songs they composed for her. But it never lasted long. Lilith's appetites always assured it.

Cat spent most of her time reading comics and keeping to herself. Sometimes boys would act interested in Cat in order to get closer to Lilith. But Cat had never been physically attracted to any of them.

She had lots of male friends, but she didn't think of them sexually. They really always seemed interested in other girls anyway and only liked her because she could carry on conversations about video games, horror movies and comic books. She'd never dated anyone and thought that maybe she just wasn't meant to be with anyone that way.

TWO

Cat didn't know at first that she was in love Lilith, it just happened over time. She found herself always wanting to be around the spider girl. It got to the point where it was actually painful to be apart from her.

Cat felt that Lilith understood her. They could talk for hours and never run out of things to say. Usually, when Cat met someone new, the person would entertain her for a while but quickly became boring. Cat found it was more interesting to read about comic book characters. But Lilith was endlessly fascinating.

Cat tried to let Lilith know that she was attracted to her. She started dressing like Lilith and listening to the same music she liked. She dyed her hair green, so she would look less plain, and wore black and white striped stockings to cover up her pasty white caterpillar legs so that they would look like Lilith's naturally candy-striped legs.

Cat's mother didn't approve of her new look. She told her that she didn't want Cat hanging out with Lilith anymore. Her mom said that Lilith had a bad reputation and you had to watch who you hung out with or you risked damaging your own. But Cat didn't care what her Mom thought. She continued to hang out with Lilith and then lied to her mother about where she was going.

However much she tried, Cat could never look like Lilith. Lilith had the body of a ballet dancer. She was muscular and limber with strong thighs and toned arms.

She liked to go dancing and mountain climbing, neither of which Cat had ever been coordinated enough to do.

Cat was awkward and had two left feet. She could never maintain good posture, and she was always knocking things over and accidently spilling her drinks. Cat figured that Lilith would never be interested in her.

THREE

One day at school, the lady bugs were teasing Cat. They spit on her and called her trash. They were always picking on her thrift store outfits even though Cat prided herself on the creativity of the fashions she designed herself.

"What are you reading, geek?" they asked Cat.

The lady bug with the most freckles, Marsha, grabbed the comic book out of Cat's hands.

"Give that back," Cat said.

"You're reading comic books? What stupid baby trash. Are you a stupid baby?"

Lilith, who happened to be passing through the hall, looked over at Cat, as if noticing her for the first time. She saw what was going on, stepped over, and said to the lady bugs, "Leave her alone."

"Ooo, the whore likes you, little caterpillar girl," Marsha said to Cat.

Lilith grabbed Marsha's hand and yanked the comic book away from her and calmly handed it back to Cat.

"Ew, don't touch me you disgusting witch. Who knows what those hands have been doing." Marsha shook the hand that Lilith had touched as if it had something disgusting on it.

After that, Lilith told Cat she thought the lady bugs were stuck up bitches. All they cared about were appearances. They judged everyone on their looks, and anyone who didn't fit in was an outcast.

Cat showed her the comic book she was reading; it was *The Invisibles* by Grant Morrison.

"*The Invisibles* is my favorite comic!" said Lilith.

"Who's your favorite character?" asked Cat.

"Lord Fanny, the Brazilian transsexual shaman, of course. Who's yours?"

"Ragged Robin, the psychic time traveling witch," said Cat.

"We're going to be great friends," Lilith said. "Like the girls in that movie, Heavenly Creatures, who bond over both of them being deformed in some way."

Lilith looked down at Cat's peeling skin.

Cat suddenly became embarrassed. She wasn't sure what Lilith meant by it. Lilith didn't seem deformed to Cat in any way at all.

FOUR

Cat ditched P.E. class to smoke a cigarette behind the gymnasium. She liked to sneak away by herself. She was always worried about getting caught, but that just added to the excitement of doing it.

As she inhaled the smoke, she felt defiant and indulgent. She heard strange noises coming from underneath the bleachers on the soccer field and walked a little closer to see what was going on.

It was Lilith. She quickened her walk, heading toward her. Cat opened her mouth to call out when she realized that Lilith wasn't alone. She was underneath the bleachers with a blue butterfly boy.

Cat had seen him around school before but she didn't remember his name. He had a black pompadour hairstyle and wore a Sisters of Mercy t-shirt with black jeans and checkerboard creepers. His wings, which looked almost too large for his body, were pierced six times on each side. A black leather D-ring dog collar circled his thin neck.

Lilith wrapped her hands around his shoulders and jumped up onto him, her strong thighs gripping his torso. He stumbled back a little, before regaining his balance as Lilith crushed her berry-colored lips against his black lipstick mouth.

She thrust her hips against his while he gripped her ass. Then she forced him down to the ground, his blue wings spreading wide beneath them like a blanket.

She fumbled with the zipper to his jeans before yanking his pants down around his ankles.

Lifting her skirt, her legs intertwined with his as she straddled him. Her long black hair veiled his face like a spider web. She gripped the back of his throat and tugged on the clasp of the dog collar, tightening it.

His indigo eyelids fluttered, his long eyelashes tickling her cheek. She kissed him on his lipstick-smeared mouth and he let out a deep moan and slid his hands up her firm belly to stroke her breasts underneath her shirt.

Cat had never seen two people have sex before. It made her feel weird, but while watching the two of them she found herself wondering what it would feel like to kiss Lilith.

She inhaled smoke slowly from her cigarette and let it roll around on her tongue imagining it as a kiss.

The boy closed his eyes. Lilith pushed her stomach harder against him and extended a long pointed appendage from her abdomen. Without the boy being aware, she gently pierced him in the chest. A thick red liquid pumped through the sharp tip and under the boy's skin.

Cat stood there motionless. The ash on the end of her cigarette grew longer and then dropped off and landed on the top of her boot. She couldn't tear her eyes away from Lilith. It was the most intimate thing she'd ever witnessed. She wasn't grossed out or afraid, even though Lilith's body was covered in blood. Lilith wore a smile unlike any Cat had ever seen her make before. There was an ecstatic look in her eyes, her skin glistened.

The blue boy's chest heaved as he struggled to breathe. His chest pulsed from navel to neck. His massive wings withered.

His body started to shrivel, drying up as all of the liquids were sucked out of him. His life drained away, into Lilith's abdomen. His eyes bulged out of his head. A thin line of dust outlined where his wings had been, a small husk like an empty chrysalis where his body was, his clothes in a heap.

Later that afternoon in Biology class, Lilith walked in and took her usual seat next to Cat. Lilith was neatly dressed, her hair was pulled back and she looked completely back to normal except Cat noticed a glittering blue piece of butterfly wing stuck to the bottom of her chin.

It hung there for a few seconds before Lilith scratched her chin and it stuck to her finger. She discretely wiped her finger on the edge of the lab table and, when she noticed Cat watching her, she gave her a conspiratorial wink.

Cat felt embarrassed, as if maybe that wink meant that Lilith knew Cat had just seen her have sex behind the bleachers.

FIVE

Cat wanted to tell Lilith about her secret crush but was too shy to actually articulate how she felt. She was also terrified that if Lilith knew that Cat was attracted to her, she would stop being her friend. So Cat started a game. She passed Lilith a note in class that said, "We do not see things as they are, we see things as we are."

Lilith smiled at the note and said, "Anais Nin?"

Cat nodded her head.

"I like it," said Lilith.

"I've left you another note in the library."

"Where?" Lilith asked.

"That's for you to discover," said Cat hoping that Lilith would be able to figure it out. Cat thought the idea of Lilith reading erotica was romantic. She had always liked playing games like this. There was only one book in the library written by Anais Nin: *The Collected Works of Erotica*.

Lilith checked out the book and inside it found a note that said "Henry Miller had an affair with Anais Nin."

Lilith had never heard of Henry Miller so she looked him up and discovered he had several books in the library. She searched through each one and in a book titled *Tropic of Cancer* she found a note in Cat's handwriting that said "Tag! You're it."

Lilith took the cue and left a note of her own inside *Tropic of Cancer* for Cat to find. When the note was answered in return by a new note appearing in the Anais

Nin book, the game had been established and the two girls exchanged quotes and messages in between classes this way on a daily basis from that point forward. Cat left Lilith notes inside *Tropic of Cancer* and Lilith left hers inside Anais Nin's book of erotica.

They always joked about how funny it would be if someone actually checked out one of those books and found their notes hidden inside.

SIX

"It's not that I don't feel bad about it," Lilith said when Cat asked her if she ever felt bad about eating the boys she had sex with, "It's just, I can't help it. It makes me feel so alive—I just lose myself in the moment, you know?"

Cat nodded her head, even though she didn't know. All she knew was that this made *her* feel alive, being with Lilith this way, weaving her long black hair into tiny braids, painting their toenails matching colors, staring up at the stars while lying in the grass next to Lilith. These were the things that made her feel alive.

SEVEN

Cat wanted to do something special for Lilith. Lilith's favorite band, Chainsaw Millipede, was coming to town. Lilith had been talking for weeks about how much she wanted to see the show but said there was no way she could afford it. Cat skipped buying lunches and babysat for her neighbor's bratty crickets so she could scrounge up enough money to buy tickets for the two of them to go to the show.

The night before the show, Cat was hanging out with Lilith in her backyard. They had made snapdragon cocktails with homemade sour orange liqueur from Lilith's mother's liquor cabinet. The air was warm and smelled like mesquite. They sat on the swings in Lilith's old swing set looking up at the stars.

"When's Chainsaw Millipede coming to town again?" Cat asked.

"Tomorrow night," Lilith said. "Why did you have to remind me? I am so bummed out that I can't go."

"What if you could go?"

"What do you mean? Do you know someone who could get us in?" Lilith's face lit up.

Cat held up the two tickets and Lilith screamed.

"Oh my god! How did you get these? These tickets cost like a fortune."

"I have my ways," Cat said, trying to sound cool.

"Ahh!! Are you for real? This is so amazing. I have always wanted to see Chainsaw Millipede live and they hardly ever tour the U.S."

Cat was beaming. She and Lilith went out together all the time to the mall and the coffee shop. But this would be different. It would be the first time that Cat had ever been to a show. Before this, Lilith had always gone to clubs with butterfly boys.

The next night, Cat made up an elaborate excuse for her mom about why she needed to borrow the car and she picked Lilith up like they were going on a date.

Lilith opened the door to her house dressed in a black leather corset that made her already tiny waist look even tinier. She had her hair up in a messy bun and wore a black knee-length pencil skirt that hugged her hips, accessorized with black stiletto ballet slippers which pointed daintily at the ends on her black and white striped legs. Cat thought she looked like a sexy secretary.

Lilith eyed Cat's outfit—a tutu skirt, striped stockings and a baggy Bauhaus t-shirt—and said, "You're not going to the show looking like *that* are you?"

Cat looked down at herself, suddenly self-conscious.

Lilith said, "Come in, I'll get you fixed up," and took her inside.

Cat had been in Lilith's bedroom many times. One time she had even spent the night and they stayed awake until morning watching Japanese anime and reading Francesca Lia Block books aloud to each other. But this time, when Lilith took Cat into her room, she felt different.

"Stand still," Lilith said, brushing out Cat's green hair with an oversized comb.

Lilith styled Cat's hair with gel and hairspray so that it stood up on her head like a hornet's nest. Then she stuck out two little black butterfly barrettes on either side of her temples. She drew spider webs around Cat's eyes with black mascara and painted her mouth with the same berry lipstick as her own.

The lipstick felt sensual, like a kiss, as Lilith slowly applied it to her top lip and then her bottom.

When Lilith was done with Cat's hair and makeup she opened a secret compartment at the bottom of her dresser revealing a stash of clothes Cat had never seen before.

"This is my collection of corsets," Lilith said, as she pulled them out and arranged them on the bed. "I don't bring them out on just any occasion because they are very expensive and mean a lot to me, but tonight feels like a special night. And I just know that one of these is going to look great on you."

There were different shapes and colors. There were under-the-bust styles and over-the-bust styles, waist trimmers, and fancy brocaded corsets lined with silk and trimmed with lace.

Lilith picked up an oily black leather corset with steel boning and a silver zipper on the front.

"I think this is the one," she said to Cat holding it out to her.

Cat took the corset from her. It was smooth and almost felt warm to the touch. It smelled like velvety mocha and peaty campfire. She wrapped it around her torso over her t-shirt and fumbled with the zipper, unable to connect it in the front.

"I don't think this will fit me," she said.

"Oh darling, don't worry. It *will* fit you. These things are designed to hold you in," Lilith said, waving her hand in the air dismissing Cat's fears.

Lilith reached around behind Cat and started to loosen

the laces on the back of the corset, adjusting it so that the bottom of the fabric rested against her hipbone. Lilith told her the corset was custom made to fit her shape by a famous corsetiere in Paris who used only finest earwig leather and narwhale boning.

Cat tugged on the sides of the leather until she could finally connect the zipper in the front. But as soon as she started zipping it, the cotton fabric of her t-shirt got caught in the teeth of the zipper.

Lilith and Cat both struggled to free the excess fabric from the jammed zipper. Cat couldn't believe that she was fucking up this special corset and worried that she had broken the zipper.

Lilith just laughed it off and said, "I think this might work better without your t-shirt."

Cat was shy about her blotchy peeling skin. The reason she liked to ditch P.E. so often was really because she didn't want anyone to see her naked. She thought Lilith would think she looked like a freak and didn't want to take her shirt off.

"I won't even look," Lilith said, reassuring her.

"But my skin is disgusting and peeling," Cat said, looking at Lilith's smooth delicately striped skin.

"Who cares about a little flakey skin?" said Lilith. "In the lighting at the club no one will even notice. Plus, you have a really cute figure and you should flaunt it."

Lilith handed Cat a hairspray bottle.

"What's this for?" Cat asked.

"Liquid encouragement," Lilith said.

"Huh?"

"It's liquor, silly. I stole it out of my mom's liquor cabinet and hid it in my hairspray bottle.

"Oh. . ." Cat said, bringing the spray bottle cautiously up to her mouth.

Cat spritzed a little of the liquid into her mouth. It tasted like air freshener. She winced and then coughed.

Lilith laughed at Cat.

"It works better if you just take the top off and drink from it."

After a couple of swigs off the hairspray bottle and some more compliments from Lilith, Cat turned around so that her back was facing Lilith and pulled off her t-shirt.

As Cat was unclasping her bra, she felt Lilith approach her from behind and reach around her wrapping the corset around Cat's body. Cat could feel Lilith's warm breath on her neck as she slid the leather against her torso, almost embracing her but not actually touching her.

Then Lilith told Cat to hold her breath and lean forward as she clasped the zipper and slowly zipped the front of the corset. Cat's nipple hardened underneath the leather when Lilith's fingers just barely grazed her breast as she pulled the zipper up to the top. Lilith didn't seem to notice but Cat felt her skin prickle and it sent a chill up her spine.

"Brace yourself against the doorframe while I tighten the laces," Lilith told her.

Cat felt like they were playing dress up and she was the doll.

Once she was laced up, Cat looked at herself in the mirror. Her waist was cinched in the center, her stomach flat as a board, and her breasts looked firmer and more voluptuous. She thought that if she were taller and her legs a little thinner she actually would look a little like Lilith. The corset felt like a second skin. She imagined she was wearing Lilith's skin and it made her feel powerful, sexy. Cat didn't care anymore that her own skin was loose and peeling because she had this new skin holding her together, embracing her, protecting her.

EIGHT

At the show, Cat and Lilith made their way to the front of the stage. The club was packed with people and there was barely any room to move. But Lilith had an effortless way of making people get out of her way. It was in the way she carried herself; her posture and natural grace.

Cat liked the way the corset restricted her movements. She felt more elegant and self-possessed. It was as if by proxy some of the spider girl's grace had rubbed off on her. She felt more confident and less shy. But she had to take shallow breaths because the corset was laced so tight, which in addition to the alcohol made her light-headed.

The lead singer of Chainsaw Millipede was a dragonfly boy wearing metal studded leather jeans, no shirt, and steel-toed combat boots. He was a few years older than Lilith and Cat, about the same age as the guys that Lilith usually went out with.

He head-banged his black liberty spikes along with his bass guitar rhythm. Upon his tattered purple-tipped dragonfly wings were sewn a patchwork of punk band logos, political statements, sigils and movie references. He had a neon pink patch on his right wing that said "kill yourself" and an Abby Hoffman quote about revolution on the other wing.

His eyes were dark and sensitive. The way he held a focused yet ambivalent gaze made it appear like he was staring straight into the eyes of every single person in the room simultaneously. His hands and arms were veined and knotted; the muscles on his chest were tight with energy and it looked like he was carving sound out of the air with his chainsaw guitar and throwing light into the audience as he bounced to the music and sang into the microphone.

Cat loved the way the music made her feel and even more than the music she loved watching Lilith dance.

The music moved through Lilith's long body as she wove patterns on the floor with her hands and feet. She craned her neck and stared up at the singer, her eyes caressing his hairless chest.

"I think patch-wing boys are the hottest," Lilith whisper-screamed into Cat's ear.

Cat nodded and Lilith stared back up at the singer. Lilith bounced around like she was catching his sound with her arms and swallowing it with her ears.

When Chainsaw Millipede played their most popular song, the crowd went wild. People were screaming out the lyrics along with them and skanking in the circle pit.

Cat had never been in a circle pit. But before she knew it, she found herself caught up in the one that spontaneously formed in front of the stage. People slammed her from every direction. They elbowed her in the chest and smashed her toes until they were bleeding in her boots.

She couldn't control her direction and spent most of her energy just trying not to get knocked down. A few times she lost her balance and thought she was going to fall over, but the people on the edge of the pit buoyed her up before she hit the ground.

Lilith slam-danced in the center of the pit, turning in circles as if she were controlling the crowd around her. She spun on one leg and then the other like a spider in the center of a web. Then she locked eyes with Cat and pointed one finger at her beckoning her to come into the center of the circle with her. Lilith wore a huge grin on her face and even though Cat was scared of the pit, Lilith's smile encouraged her to jump through, get knocked down and around until she reached center.

In the middle of the swirling group of dancers, Cat found the calm at the center of the storm. The spider girl grabbed onto her and held her tightly. Their shiny leather corsets rubbed together making their torsos stick and Cat felt for a moment like she was a part of Lilith, moving as she moved, effortlessly.

Cat's body tingled. She could feel heat rising in her face and thought her skin was going to flare up again. Her heart pounded like the bass in the speakers.

Lilith's face looked like an H.R. Giger painting in the greenish glow of the club. Dancing in the center of the circle as the crowd bounced in frantic chaos around them, the caterpillar girl never felt more alive. Cat knew in that moment that she wanted to be with Lilith forever. She never wanted to be apart from her. She felt safe and powerful when she was with Lilith.

As the song ended, they spun around, facing each other. Their hips pressed gently against one another. They locked eyes. Cat wanted to kiss Lilith. Confidence rose within her and she felt capable of anything.

She leaned in toward Lilith's face, eyes lowering toward the spider girl's ripe blackberry lips. Tilting her head, she puckered her mouth.

But just as she was about to connect, Lilith turned her head and Cat's kiss landed awkwardly on Lilith's cheek. Lilith was looking over her shoulder at a red-winged butterfly boy who put his hand on her back.

"Kas, how are you!" Lilith said turning around and hugging the butterfly boy.

Cat didn't know what to do. Did Lilith think it was weird that she had kissed her? Did she even notice?

Cat stood there for a few seconds waiting to see if Lilith would acknowledge her, or say anything, or even look at her. But Lilith was turned the other way, flirting with Kas. She touched him on the shoulder, staring in his eyes and laughing at the inaudible phrases he shouted over the noise of the crowd.

Then the band started their next song and the crowd began slamming again.

Before she could say anything to Lilith, Cat got knocked to the ground by an ant boy's knee and a beefy Cockroach dude stepped on her fingers crushing them under his thick-soled boot causing crippling pain to shoot up Cat's arm. She screamed out, but the guy didn't even notice her and no one else paid any attention to her either.

Lilith had completely forgotten about her and was dancing with the butterfly boy. His red wings fluttered in a swirling motion around him. His hands caressed the curve of Lilith's hip.

Cat scrambled to her feet and stuck her crushed fingers into her mouth to soothe herself and then forced her way through the crowd all the way out to the lobby where the bathrooms were located.

A long line queued in front of the women's room, and Cat couldn't handle the thought of waiting in it. She noticed a couple of other impatient girls walk shamelessly into the men's room where there was no line. Cat thought about following them but was too shy.

She wanted to escape, to be somewhere she could be alone. The night was ruined. She couldn't believe that she had embarrassed herself like that.

After getting all the way through the line to the bathroom, the show was almost over and Cat couldn't stand the idea of going back into the room to watch Lilith dance with the butterfly boy. She felt stupid for daring to think she could kiss Lilith. She wanted to rewind time and erase the awkward moment between them. Instead, she went outside and waited through the rest of the show in her mom's car.

Lilith came out of the club clutching onto Kas's shoulder and giggling. Cat was leaning against her car smoking a cigarette. Lilith walked straight over to Cat and gave her a hug. Cat was relieved to see her and to feel her in her arms. As she hugged her she thought maybe things weren't going to be any different between them after all, maybe Lilith thought it was completely normal for Cat to kiss her on the cheek while they were dancing. But then she heard Lilith whisper in her ear.

"Thanks for waiting, but I won't be needing a ride home. Kas is going to take me for a ride on his motorcycle."

Cat felt rejected. She had spent all her money on these tickets, her toes were bleeding, and she had just spent the last hour waiting at the car for Lilith who was now running off with this guy she just met.

"Are you sure?" asked Cat.

"Don't worry about me," Lilith answered and winked at her.

Kas grabbed Lilith by the waist and pulled her away toward his motorcycle. Cat felt like her heart had been stomped on.

NINE

Over the weekend, Cat spent most of her time obsessing about what had happened. She was worried that the next time she saw Lilith things were going to be weird and she didn't want anything to mess up their friendship. But she also couldn't control the feelings she had every time she was around Lilith.

She still had Lilith's corset.

She closed her eyes and rubbed her hands along the smooth leather imagining it was Lilith's skin. She caressed the leather with one hand and reached down between her legs with her other, rubbing the knuckle of her thumb against her clit through her wet panties.

Imagining the shape of Lilith's body, she ran her fingertips along the boning of the leather corset. Her flesh turned hot and cold and the skin on her back shifted and changed shape.

She looked in the mirror at her naked body and saw her back was covered in red welts where her skin had stretched. Wings started to form. The loose skin on her back became thicker and molded into two bulges just beneath her skin that were tender and hurt when she poked them.

TEN

Lilith came to school wearing a dress made from red butterfly wings. It looked like couture fashion that should be on a runway in Paris. A lot of people complimented her on it, telling her the wings looked so realistic. The girls all gossiped about how they thought that she'd probably made her skirt out of real butterfly wings. Most of them didn't really believe it was true, but the anti-arachnid kids thought it was disgusting. They called it inhumane and told her she should be ashamed of herself.

Cat could tell that Lilith didn't care what anyone thought. It was obvious the spider girl knew she looked hot in the outfit she'd created and there wasn't anything anyone could say about it that would change her mind. Cat loved that about her.

"I wanted to apologize for the awkwardness on Friday night," Cat said when she saw her in Biology class. "I just wanted you to know that I. . ."

"No, no don't even worry about it," Lilith said. "I should have made it clear earlier in the night that if I met anyone I probably wouldn't need a ride home."

Cat could tell that Lilith didn't know what she meant. Cat wasn't talking about the ride situation—she was worried about the kiss.

"Kas was incredible by the way," said Lilith. "He tasted like raspberries . . . Oh and his bike was awesome. He drove me out to this bonfire party in the middle of the desert where there were dozens of hot butterfly boys. We danced and drank tequila and talked all night long." She licked her lips. "It was one of the best nights of my life."

Cat decided to change the topic.

"What did you get for the answer to number seven on the math homework?" Cat asked.

"Math homework? Oh shit! I completely forgot about it. You don't mind if I copy yours, do you?"

Cat sighed and handed over her completed homework.

ELEVEN

Cat wore Lilith's corset to school every day underneath her clothes. She looked at herself in the mirror as she was getting ready and knew that no one would be able to tell. She liked having this secret. Her posture was straighter because she found that it was impossible to slouch in a corset and she noticed that boys kept staring at her breasts.

Lilith sat up on a tree branch in their usual lunch spot. Her stuff was scattered across the ground under the tree and Cat noticed a scrap of green butterfly wing stuck to the inside of Lilith's purse like a used tissue. She was talking to Paulette and eating a sausage sandwich. When Cat came over, Paulette offered her half of her sandwich, even though she should have known that Cat didn't eat stuff like that.

"I don't eat sausage, remember?"

"Oh that's right, you're a vegan," said Paulette

"Not a vegan, I just don't eat cooked food."

Cat only ate raw fruits and vegetables because she thought it was gross to eat anything that wasn't alive.

"You look like you've lost weight," Lilith said to Cat. "That diet must be working for you."

Cat felt her face turn red. She shrugged.

Lilith jumped down off the tree and came over to Cat.

"No seriously," Lilith said, "you look great. What's your secret?"

Cat looked down at her feet. "Nothing."

"And your waist has gotten so tiny," Lilith said, reaching out and squeezing the side of Cat's stomach.

Lilith's eyes widened when she felt the corset. Then a big smile broke out on her face.

Cat was mortified. She knew that Lilith felt the stiffness of her corset through her t-shirt. She was afraid that Lilith was going to laugh at her and tell everyone that she was wearing a corset.

But instead, Lilith patted her stomach and whispered in her ear, "I sometimes like to wear that one, so I'm going to need that back from you."

Cat was embarrassed. She knew that she was going to have to give the corset back to Lilith. She hadn't intended on keeping it so long, but she'd not mentioned it because subconsciously she didn't want to give it back to her.

"Yes, of course," said Cat.

Lilith smiled at her and said, "You have been looking good lately. Your skin really looks like it's clearing up."

Cat couldn't decide if that was a compliment or not. She worried that Lilith thought she was a freak and was just trying not to embarrass her out of politeness.

TWELVE

Cat woke up the next day with her head between her legs. Muscles tight. Sore back. Cramps in her abdomen like knife blades stabbing her from inside. Charlie horses seized the muscles in both her legs. She couldn't see. A foggy haze blocked her vision.

She reached her hands to her face and the lumps on her back cracked open oozing oily liquid. The skin on her neck loosened as she stretched forward. Her spine cracked like a xylophone, the haze cleared from her eyes and wings unfolded from around her body.

She stretched out her new muscles. They were strong and full of energy. She circled her neck and lengthened her spine. Wiggling her antennae, she reached back with her fingertips and touched the wings. Oily residue from the metamorphosis coated her nails as she scratched the bits of dead skin off the slick surface of each side.

Like a blooming flower, she widened her wings, stretching them out as far as they would go. Tall and shimmering, they doubled her size. Turquoise blue and translucent as the Mediterranean Ocean. Delicate veins laced each wing in thin black spiral patterns and small yellow dots that looked like miniature skulls decorated her shoulders.

She looked down at her new shape and admired her upward turned breasts, her shapely hips, her long lean limbs. She stood in front of the full-length mirror on her bedroom wall and spun around, bending over to inspect herself from every angle.

She felt beautiful. Her heart was on fire. This was what she had been waiting for. No more peeling skin, no more strange lumps and thick doughy legs. She was finally a butterfly.

THIRTEEN

Freddy Centipede was throwing a party that night and everyone at school was invited. He was one of the richest and most popular boys at school. His parents had a giant mansion on the side of a cliff overlooking the valley. Cat normally didn't like Freddie's parties but Lilith had been trying to convince her to go for weeks. When she imagined the look on Lilith's face watching her arrive for the first time in butterfly form, Cat decided to go.

She spent all day getting ready, doing her hair in different styles, deciding what to wear. After discarding about two dozen outfits she decided to go with a black minidress that Lilith had picked out for her that she had never worn because she thought it was too revealing. Her new wings stuck out the back of the strapless dress like blue dragon flowers. She added red plaid thigh-high stockings with vintage button garters. Then strapped herself into 32-buckle platform boots that came up to her knees. She affixed a pair of vintage goggles to her head in front of her antennas to complete the look.

Everyone was at the party. All the popular kids, unpopular kids, geeks, freaks and jocks. People kept staring at Cat. She could tell they were shocked by her appearance. It always fascinated people to discover what type of butterflies the caterpillars became.

This time, Cat didn't mind that they were looking at her. She had always been the weird outcast geek that no one really paid any attention to. Now, everyone gawked at her like she was some kind of celebrity. She felt ready to show everyone, especially Lilith, what she always knew she was like on the inside. But where was Lilith?

Cat searched for the spider girl but it didn't seem like she was at the party yet. So she wandered around enjoying the way her body moved. She felt taller, more graceful. She heard people whispering her name under their breath, but could tell by their smiles that they were only admiring her.

A swimming pool took up a big portion of the backyard with a fire pit on one end of it. Large flower-shaped sculptures lined the patio that looked out onto the lights of the city below.

Cat imagined what it would be like to fly over the city with her new pair of wings. But the most she was able to do was hover.

She found some of her friends in the kitchen drinking cans of PBR and passing a bong.

"Oh my god," Paulette squealed when she saw Cat. "You've turned! Let me see, let me see." Paulette jumped in circles around Cat. She tugged on the end of one of Cat's wings pulling it out from her body so she could inspect the pattern.

Cat stretched her wings out so that Paulette could get a better look at her. A crowd circled around Cat.

"You look absolutely beautiful," Paulette said. The moth girl reached out a finger and touched the yellow skull-freckles on Cat's shoulder. Her touch made the skin on her wings vibrate and ripple. "And I *love* your outfit."

"You look hot," said Larry, exhaling a cloud of smoke under his heavily lidded dome-shaped slug eyes.

"Thanks you guys," said Cat feeling really good about

herself for the first time in a long time.

One of the popular jock beetles from her algebra class waved from across the room. And the butterfly boy from A.P. English said, "Hey Cat," even though he hadn't spoken to her all year outside of the one time he asked to borrow her flash drive. Cat wondered if Lilith thought he was attractive.

Then she saw Lilith walk through the front door. Cat almost didn't recognize her. Lilith's hair was pulled back into an elaborate up-do like a samurai warrior princess. Her face was painted white with black symbols drawn on her eyelids.

A purple-winged butterfly boy ran over to Lilith and circled his arm around her corseted waist. The corset had a red hourglass emblem painted on the front of it like the abdomen of a black widow.

Cat couldn't wait to see Lilith's reaction to her butterfly wings. She waited for Lilith to look across the room and notice her, but instead, Lilith followed the butterfly boy in the other direction.

Cat went after them but was blocked by the crowd and lost sight of where they went. Freddy's mansion was huge.

"Have you seen Lilith?" Cat asked everyone she passed. They were all either too drunk to understand her or would say, "Yes, she was just here," and then look around blankly.

She searched behind closed doors and behind one of them she accidentally found two cicada boys having sex. The high-pitched sound of their voices was deafening and it looked like one of them was shedding his skin. Cat closed the door quickly and decided to only check the common areas.

Finally, she gave up and returned to the kitchen where Paulette and Larry were still passing a bong and Lilith walked in behind her.

"I've been looking all over for you!" Cat said to Lilith.

"I didn't know you were coming," Lilith said.

Cat stood in front of Lilith, expecting her to make some type of comment about her butterfly wings but she didn't. Instead she just went on like normal talking about some guy.

After pretending to listen for a few minutes, Cat said, "Great outfit."

"Yours too," Lilith replied.

"I like your shoes," Cat said, looking down at Lilith's Fluevog heels.

"Thanks," said Lilith.

Cat waited for something more. But instead of commenting on her metamorphosis, Lilith said, "Where's the booze?" and bent down opening an ice chest by the refrigerator.

Lilith grabbed a can of PBR and walked outside. Cat followed her. The swimming pool had a glass edge alongside the cliff and looked like it was a part of the horizon. Some mosquito boys were skimming the surface of the water with hockey sticks, whacking a beach ball. Two spotlights at the bottom of the pool illuminated the water, making the mosquitos' wings shimmer.

Lady bug girls in bikinis lay out on the lounge chairs even though it was nighttime. A group of boys stood off to the side watching the girls. The ladybugs pretended to ignore the boys.

Marsha's hair spiraled up in a beehive do that looked like something out of a 1950's Hollywood film. She wore oversized white sunglasses and a bikini that highlighted her petite ladybug curves.

As Cat walked by, the ogling boys turned their eyes on her. It felt weird to have people noticing her. Lilith was usually the one everyone was looking at.

Lilith seemed preoccupied with other things. She scanned the patio watching the partiers. Cat started to wonder what might be wrong with her. She thought Lilith would have said more about her wings. Maybe Lilith didn't like the way that she turned out.

"I was thinking about getting my wings pierced," Cat said, trying to draw Lilith's attention to them.

"I've always thought about getting something pierced," said Lilith wistfully.

"What would you get?"

"I don't know, I was thinking maybe my lip or my eyebrows. But it might be fun to get my nipples pierced."

Cat pictured in her mind what Lilith's nipples would look like pierced. It turned her on.

"Yeah, that would be hot," she said, biting her lower lip.

Lilith smiled and put her hands on her hips.

Cat studied her mouth and her eyebrows. She imagined sucking on Lilith's pierced lips and pulling on her eyebrows. She felt herself start to blush.

"Who was that guy you were with earlier?" Cat asked.

"Oh, Tyler?"

"That was Tyler?" Cat asked. "Caterpillar Tyler?"

"He just turned. Doesn't he look incredible? His wings are like rose petals."

Cat's stomach sank. Lilith must only be attracted to butterfly boys. She'd not even mentioned Cat's wings. Cat stretched out her wings and leaned forward pretending to adjust the buckle on her boot, hoping to capture Lilith's attention.

Lilith crushed her beer can and said, "I'm gonna get another drink, do you want one?"

Cat looked up at her.

"No," she said, coldly.

Lilith shrugged and walked back toward the kitchen. Cat watched her through the window. She laughed and drank and flirted with the butterfly boys. One of them came over to her and she grabbed the loose flesh on his elbow, yanking him toward her and pressing her mouth to his throat. Cat couldn't watch anymore. She wanted nothing more than to be with Lilith. She had waited all of this time in the hope that once she became a butterfly Lilith would want her, but now she could see she was wrong.

FOURTEEN

When Lilith came back out she found Cat on a bench by the swimming pool away from the rest of the party. Cat had tears in her eyes, wiping them away as Lilith approached.

"What's going on with you tonight?" Lilith asked. "Why have you been avoiding me?"

"Me avoiding *you*?" Cat said. "You are the one that's been avoiding *me*."

Cat tried to act normal like nothing was bothering her, but her eyes welled up again when she looked at Lilith.

"Shh, it's okay." Lilith came over to her and put her arm around Cat's shoulders. "Tell me what's wrong."

Lilith's embrace was painful for Cat. The feeling of the spider girl's arm around her made Cat imagine what she could never have.

"I can't," said Cat.

"Does it have to do with your transformation?" Lilith asked.

Cat looked at her. It was the first time that Lilith had even acknowledged her transformation.

"It has everything to do with that," Cat whispered.

"What do you mean?"

"I thought you would notice me," Cat said. "I thought once I became a butterfly you would think I was beautiful."

Lilith looked deeply into her eyes. "I have always thought you were beautiful, Cat. Once you changed, I just saw more of who I already knew you were."

Cat started to tear up again, but this time it was from happiness.

"Remember the corset that I lent you?" Lilith asked.

"Yes," Cat said sheepishly.

"After I found out that you were wearing it under your clothes, I kept imagining you that way. I liked that you enjoyed wearing it. I thought it was totally sexy."

"Oh my god, I was so embarrassed about that!" Cat said.

"And you look great tonight," Lilith said. "I'm so happy to see you finally feeling good about yourself. Why do you care what I think anyway? You know you look hot. I've seen the way people are looking at you."

Cat felt different knowing that Lilith thought she was hot.

"I thought that things would be different." Cat paused and looked down at her hands. She lowered her voice and in barely a whisper she said, "I thought things would be different between *us*."

Lilith didn't respond. Cat started to sweat. She knew that if she didn't tell Lilith how she felt about her she would burst.

"It's hard for me to talk about it because we are such good friends," Cat said. "And the last thing that I would want to do is mess up our friendship. In fact, I have been terrified to tell you this because I am afraid of what you will think of me. I don't want to lose you as a friend."

Cat didn't want to look at Lilith's face. She was afraid of seeing her expression. She was afraid of being rejected.

"Lilith, I'm in love with you."

Lilith was silent for what seemed like a long time to Cat but was really only a few seconds. Cat felt all the air go out of her chest. Then Lilith touched Cat's chin with her palm and turned her face toward her, forcing Cat to look her in the eyes.

"I love you, too," Lilith said in a sweet voice like the one she would use to speak to a child or a puppy-fly.

Cat felt her heart sink. She had to make it clear to Lilith what she meant.

"I don't just mean that I love you, I mean that I am attracted to you."

Lilith's expression didn't change.

"Please don't hate me," Cat said.

"I don't hate you." Lilith took her arm off of Cat's shoulder and took her by the hands. "I'm attracted to you, too."

"Wait, what?" Cat said. "Are you just saying that?"

Lilith smiled. "I've always been into you. Even before we met, I used to check you out every time that we ran into each other at lunch."

Cat couldn't believe what she was hearing.

"You used to check me out?" Cat said, arching her eyebrows in surprise.

Lilith laughed. "Yeah, is that so hard to believe?"

"But I thought you were just interested in boys."

"I am interested in boys. But with them, it's just sex. With you it's different. It goes deeper than that. You are my best friend. And you are the cutest chick I know. Just look at you." Lilith stroked her finger along Cat's wing.

Cat shivered.

"I love these skull-freckles," said Lilith.

"Why didn't you ever let on that you were interested in me?" Cat asked.

"You know why . . . It's awkward. I thought that you would be afraid that I would eat you."

Lilith's eyes consumed Cat. She was sucked into them

like two vortexes and for the first time she saw what she'd been longing to see. Lilith was telling her the truth. She was attracted to Cat. Her stomach knotted up. Her breath caught in her throat.

Lilith leaned in toward Cat and put her hand on her cheek. She brushed a lock of hair out of her eyes and pulled Cat's face toward hers.

The kiss was a magical crazy starlight popcorn filled explosion. Cat's tongue was sucked in the spider girl's mouth, sharp fangs caressed its curve. Every muscle in her body relaxed. She felt like she was floating. She couldn't believe it had finally happened. She closed her eyes.

A cricket boy stumbled into them, splashing beer on the toes of Lilith's shoes.

"Hey, watch it," Lilith said to him.

"Whoa, were you two just making out?" The boy said, stumbling sideways.

"It's none of your business," Lilith said, turning her body to face him.

"Hey, it's cool. I'm totally into it. If you want, I'd be happy to join in."

"Fuck off, asshole," said Lilith

"Lesbian bitch," the cricket boy said and stumbled drunkenly around the pool looking like he was about to fall in at any moment.

"Can we go someplace more private?" Cat said, suddenly aware of where she was and who might be watching.

"Jerk," Lilith said, turning back to Cat.

"I noticed the back gate was unlocked," Cat said, pointing behind them to fence at the end of the patio covered in darkness.

FIFTEEN

The two girls sneaked into the desert behind the fence at the cliff's edge holding hands and helping each other over the rocks. They brought a blanket and two bottles of strawberry wine cooler. Laughter, music, and all the sounds of the party still raged in the background.

Lilith spread the blanket on a soft sandy spot between two mesquite trees. She and Cat took off their shoes and stretched out on their stomachs. A tingle of expectation buzzed between them. Cat knew where she wanted things to go, but she didn't know if it would actually happen.

Cat fluttered her wings and rose a few feet into the air. Lilith flipped over onto her back and looked up at Cat. The butterfly girl dangled her plaid toes above Lilith and they both started to laugh. Lilith hugged Cat around the legs and pulled her down to the ground again.

"Don't fly away from me," said Lilith.

Cat melted into Lilith's arms. The spider girl held her close and kissed her neck. Snuggling her head against Cat's chest, she closed her eyes.

Cat kissed the black symbols drawn on Lilith's eyelids, marking them with lipstick rings like a bull's-eye. She caressed Lilith's muscular arms, feeling shy about touching her body anywhere else.

Lilith stroked Cat's green hair, winding her fingers through it, tugging slightly. She licked the skulls on Cat's shoulder and ran her sharp teeth along the edge of her ear.

"You taste like Halloween candy," she whispered, her hot breath raising the hair on Cat's arms.

Cat flickered with anticipation. She felt wetness spread between her thighs. Without speaking, Lilith slowly unzipped her corset in front of Cat. The spider girl's dark nipples hardened in the cool night air. They looked like they were stained with blood. She removed Cat's dress, unbuttoned her garters and peeled her stockings off one at a time, kissing Cat's legs, and tickling the back of her knees. After shedding the rest of their clothes, they lay naked together under the stars.

Lilith took Cat's hand and brought it to her breast, tracing her nipples with Cat's fingers. Cat climbed on top of the spider girl, straddling her, and pressed down on her shoulders with the palms of her hands. She spread her wings, creating a canopy above them. Lilith stared up with eyes like burning stars. Even though Cat had Lilith pinned to the blanket, the butterfly girl felt that the spider could eat her at any moment.

She waited for Lilith to respond, to throw her off or pull her close but the spider girl just lay there staring up at her.

"What's wrong?" Cat asked, feeling self-conscious.

"Nothing," said Lilith, nuzzling her head against Cat's arm.

"Why aren't you getting into it?" Cat asked.

"I am into it," Lilith said stroking her forehead.

"But not like with the boys."

"Boys are different." Lilith smiled and took a sip of her wine cooler. "What do you want me to do?"

"I want you to *want* me."

"I *do* want you," said Lilith. "I want you so much. But I have to hold myself back. I don't want to get carried away and go too far."

"I'm not worried about that," Cat said. "I want you to make love to me with all of your passion."

Lilith gazed deep into Cat's eyes and stroked her hair. The butterfly girl's eyes were pleading.

Lilith reached up and kissed her deeply. Her mouth tasted like strawberries and alcohol. In the middle of the kiss, she grabbed Cat's hair and flipped over on top of her. She paused and took another sip of her wine cooler. She didn't swallow it. She brought her lips to Cat's and let the liquid slide from her tongue down the butterfly girl's throat.

Lilith slowly lowered herself down the length of Cat's body, kissing her neck and shoulders. She reached her nipples and took another sip of her wine cooler. She placed her lips over Cat's nipple and sucked. The liquid swirled around Cat's areola. Cold. Stimulating.

The strawberry liquid slid between Cat's breasts and pooled in her belly button. Lilith lapped the liquid from Cat's center, slurping it up through her conical shaped tongue. Then she lowered her head between Cat's legs.

"I want to taste you," said Lilith, licking her lips.

Thighs wet with butterfly nectar, strawberry wine cooler, and spit. Lilith drew spirals across Cat's clitoris with her tongue, sending waves of heat through her body.

Cat stretched her arms out above her head and elongated her spine. Spreading her legs wider, she invited Lilith's tongue between the folds of her vulva. She ground her hips against Lilith's face, pushing her deeper with her hands.

Lilith came up for air and smiled at her hungrily, baring her fangs and licking her chin. The look in her eyes was suddenly wild, ferocious.

When Cat saw that hungry look in Lilith's eyes, the

muscles inside her pelvis tightened. Her skin tingled. It was the same look Lilith had the time she ate the butterfly boy under the bleachers.

"Why are you looking at me like that?" Cat asked, the spider girl's face between her quivering thighs.

Lilith stared deeply into Cat. Her eyes were on fire. Cat could see the lust burning behind them.

"Are you going to eat me?" Cat asked in a shaky tone.

Lilith realized what she was doing and shook her head, trying to shake the hunger away.

"I'm sorry," said the spider girl. "I didn't mean to get carried away."

"It's okay," Cat said.

"I would never do that with you."

Cat broke eye contact. Suddenly, she felt rejected. Her eyes began to water.

Then she said, "Why not?"

Lilith giggled. "What do you mean *why not?*"

"I thought you loved me," Cat said.

"I *do* love you," Lilith said.

"Then why won't you eat me?"

Lilith stared back at her in disbelief.

"What are you talking about, Cat? You're my best friend."

"You ate all of those butterfly boys. I want you to love me like you loved them." Cat wiped tears from her cheeks. "I want you to eat me."

"No way," Lilith said.

"But you have to!"

"You mean too much to me."

Then something snapped inside of Cat's butterfly brain. She lunged forward.

"Eat me," Cat screamed, forcing herself against Lilith, probing at her belly searching for the extra appendage that would inject the poison. "I *need* you to do it."

Lilith's appendage started to emerge. She couldn't help herself from getting turned on. She had never been with anyone so insistent.

"Don't," Lilith whispered.

"Put it inside me," Cat said, pulling on the stinger.

Cat slid her clitoris up against Lilith's stinger. She felt a drop of poison slip out the tip and numb the skin around her vulva.

Then Cat reached down and guided the stinger inside her vagina. It felt hard and sharp.

"Okay, just for a minute," Lilith gasped as the stinger slipped inside. "Then I'll pull out."

She thrust herself against the butterfly girl.

Lilith and Cat fucked under the stars. They screamed like cicadas and slammed their bodies against one another.

As Lilith was about to pull out, Cat locked her legs around Lilith's thighs. She held her inside.

"Do it," Cat said as she pictured being stabbed in the abdomen. Cat wanted to orgasm but she stopped herself, holding out for the actual moment. She opened her eyes and looked at Lilith.

"Let me out," Lilith screamed.

"Suck me dry," Cat said.

"No," Lilith struggled to free herself, but Cat's thighs had grown strong and held firm. She pushed Cat, trying to get away but it just made Cat more excited. Lilith started to cry.

"I don't want to kill you," Lilith sobbed. "I love you too much."

She could no longer contain herself and exploded in poisonous orgasm. Cat felt Lilith's essence spread through her. Every muscle in her body convulsed. Her breath quickened. Her wings felt stiff.

With fading strength, she pushed Lilith's body back down to her crotch and shoved herself against the spider girl's mouth. Lilith, lost in her own orgasm, could no longer resist.

Cat looked down as Lilith lapped the red fluid oozing out of her vagina. She couldn't tell if it was her blood, the poison, or her insides melting away. She smiled as she looked into Lilith's eyes.

Tears streamed down the spider girl's face as she hungrily sunk her fangs into Cat's stiffening flesh.

"It's okay," Cat whispered, brushing the tears from Lilith's cheeks. "It's what I've always wanted."

Cat's orgasm came in waves, surging forth from her pelvis. She arched her back and her skin pulsed as Lilith sucked the fluid from between her legs. She felt the moisture being drawn out of her and her skin start to wither.

Lilith sobbed and gripped her friend's hands. She could no longer pull herself away, her tears mixing with the red goo oozing forth between her lips until the butterfly girl crumbled to dust and drifted away.

CLOCKWORK GIRL

ONE

The clockwork girl felt the box scratch the top of her head and the bottom of her toes as the cardboard shifted around her. Even in the light of her breast's glowing filament, all she could see was the cardboard in front of her nose. She imagined faces staring back at her in the swirl-patterned paper. Zipties bound her ankles and wrists to the box. She couldn't move but she could still imagine. She had lost all concept of time. The faces she imagined scared her.

"Open this one next," said a woman's voice.

"Be careful with that, it's fragile," said another, deeper voice.

The box started to shake.

"Don't shake it. I said, it's fragile."

Scratching noises near her stomach. The clockwork girl blinked, adjusting her lenses to the brightly lit room as the box was torn apart. Beams of colored light glittered against her metal skin. Lying on her back, strapped into the box, all she could see was the high ceiling, its warm orange paint and dark wooden beams, the tip of a Christmas tree, a corn-husk angel on top. Then a girl's face. It was the first real face she had ever known. She instantly loved that face, jet black hair, big brown eyes.

"What is it?" said the girl, turning to her parents.

"A companion for you. A clockwork girl," said the mother.

"Holy shit! You got a tick-tock," said her brother.

The girl stroked her silver painted fingernails slowly across the etched brass skin of the clockwork girl, her light bulb breasts, her oval belly. The clockwork girl felt an electric pulse through her body as she was touched. The black-haired girl looked at her tenderly. It was as if she knew what was going through the clockwork girl's mind, how afraid and alone she felt locked inside the box. The young girl took out a pocket knife and slashed the zipties.

"This is a big responsibility," said the mother, "but your father and I feel you're ready. Don't let us down."

"She's a slave. You can make her do whatever you want," said the brother.

"She's a person?" said the girl.

"She is a toy, like your doggie," said the father.

"That means, inside, she's a real girl . . ."

"No, not anymore. Only her brain is human. They remove the brains from less fortunate girls and put them into mechanical bodies, transforming them into very special toys for nice privileged girls such as yourself. It's very sophisticated technology, and very expensive."

"This is wrong . . ." said the girl.

"Marisol, be grateful to your father. If it were not for him you would not have all of the wonderful toys that you have," said the mother.

"But I don't want a human toy, it's not right. She's a person."

The father gave Marisol a stern look and she knew better than to keep talking. The girl's brother snickered.

"Would anyone like some buñuelos de viento?" said the mother. She lifted her hand slowly and waved with one finger to the maid standing in the corner of the room holding a tray of Christmas cookies. Her finger drooped under the weight of a giant amber scarab ring.

The room was warm and festive. Christmas lights hung in the arched doorways. The smell of fresh tamales and arroz con pollo filled the air. Poinsettia flowers as big as patio umbrellas lined the walls. Servants stood in the wings holding platters of champagne and ready to assist if anything was needed. In the center of the room was a large tree with gifts clustered around the base. None of the boxes were as big as the one that the clockwork girl had emerged from.

Marisol took one of the cookies that her mother offered. It was shaped like a snowflake and just as delicate. She held it out to the clockwork girl. Marisol's brown eyes told the clockwork girl she should take it, but before she could move the mother snatched it from her hands.

"Ah! No food. She doesn't need that, she just needs winding," said the mother.

"Yes, it is very important that you wind her each day," said the father.

"She doesn't eat or sleep, the clockwork keeps her alive. But you must be certain to wind her each day or she will die," said the mother. She placed the cookie back on the tray where it crumbled into powdered sugar dust and she waved the maid away. "But never mind that right now. Come, open some more of your presents."

The girl glanced over at the stack of brightly wrapped boxes under the tree and her brother climbing amongst them, shaking each one next to his ear. Then Marisol looked back at the clockwork girl. She had a large key on her back like fairy wings. Marisol reached out and took the clockwork girl's hand in her own, and the doll smiled at her.

"We have to take her back to the factory. I can't believe that you thought that turning a human girl into a toy for me was a good idea. It is sick and wrong."

"Marisol Yvonne Reyes-Jimenez, don't talk to your father that way," said her mother.

"We are not taking her back," said the father.

"Why not?"

"Because I said so. Do you know how many children are begging their parents for toys like this? Don't you understand how good you have it? Stop being an ungrateful brat and open the rest of your gifts," said the father.

"You aren't listening to me. I am telling you that we have to help this poor girl. What you've done to her isn't right and there's no way I am keeping a girl as a toy."

"She's not a girl anymore, she's clockwork. This is a very special model, one of a kind. Not just anyone can get one of these. Once you show her off to all your friends you'll be thanking me that you have such a generous father who gives you nice things."

Marisol opened her mouth to say something but the mother gripped her by the knee and whispered, "If you want to help her then you will take care of her. This is what I mean by responsibility. If we take her back to the factory she will be disassembled. She will die."

Ignoring her mother, Marisol led the clockwork girl out of the room by tugging on her arm. The toy girl's hip joints squeaked quietly as she walked, the clockwork gears in her chest ticked a little faster.

TWO

The toy room was two levels high. The first floor was a labyrinth of hallways leading into smaller chambers, each decorated with unique themes. The upper level had a glass floor so Marisol could peer down into each of the rooms below like a giant doll house.

There was a Japanese animation room decorated pink, filled with dolls with big eyes and funny cute stuffed animals; a pony room with toy ponies of every size and color; an aquatic room where the walls on all four sides were aquariums filled with tropical fish; a tea party room straight out of Alice in Wonderland; a dress-up room filled with costumes; a book room; and many others. The ceiling of the second level was a large dome upon which danced an image of the night sky like a planetarium.

The clockwork girl followed Marisol up to the second level, her brass feet clicking along the glass floor.

"What is your name?" Marisol asked the clockwork girl.

The doll stared back at her blankly, her eyes spun like bicycle wheels.

"What were you called before you were turned into a doll?"

"I don't know," said the clockwork girl, her voice like a theramin, "I don't remember anything before the toy shop. In the toy shop, I wasn't called anything."

"Well, you need a name. How about I call you Lucilla?"

The clockwork girl frowned.

"Okay, how about Marcella?"

The clockwork girl tilted her head to the left with a squeak and said, "Definitely not."

"So what should I call you?" asked Marisol.

The clockwork girl looked down, she was standing above the aquatic room and she could see baby sharks circling in the tank below her feet.

"Pichi," she said.

Marisol laughed, "Okay, Pichi."

Pichi clapped her hands together and smiled, the sound of her hands clapping like cymbals. Then she was suddenly knocked off of her feet, something slamming into her from behind, and she toppled face-first into the glass. The baby sharks scattered beneath her.

"Maki!" Marisol yelled.

Pichi rolled over and came face to face with a giant drooling dog. Marisol ran over behind the dog and pulled it back by one of the spring links in its neck. The dog had gray fluffy fur covering its face and eyes. Its neck was a giant coiled spring. The dog's body was a patchwork amalgam of different types of fur, some long and some short, all different colors. From its body four more springs extended, acting as legs, and its tail was a wagging antenna. Pichi was scared for a moment but encouraged by the way the dog submitted under Marisol's strength.

"Don't mind Maki," Marisol said, "he's super friendly once he gets to know people."

Pichi got to her feet and carefully approached the dog. He sniffed her fingers and the sensation of his whiskers made the tiny lights on her knuckles flicker.

Marisol took Pichi to an empty room in the labyrinth.

She told the clockwork girl that it would be her room and she would help her decorate it however she wanted.

"No sharks," said Pichi.

"Okay, you got it," said Marisol. She smiled, "We are going to be best friends."

"Time for bed," Marisol's mother said from the doorway to the toy room.

Marisol hooked her arm through Pichi's and the two girls walked out to meet the mother.

"Pichi is coming to bed with me," said Marisol.

"Toys must stay in the toy room," said the mother. "You know that."

"But she'll get lonely," said Marisol.

"She's just a toy, she doesn't get lonely," said the mother. She took Marisol's arm and carefully pulled it away from the clockwork girl.

"Goodnight Pichi," Marisol called after her, as the mother dragged the daughter down the hallway. "Maki will keep you company."

Pichi walked back to her empty room and lay on the floor, staring up at the blue twinkling night sky through her glass ceiling until Maki came across the second level and sat on top of the room, blocking her view.

THREE

"Keep your eyes closed," Marisol said. The clockwork girl sat still while Marisol wound her up. "I'm almost done."

Pichi could feel the springs inside herself tightening like a corset as Marisol turned her key. The turning slowed and the clockwork girl felt Marisol brace her feet against something on the floor in order to gain the leverage necessary to complete the final few turns.

This was the game that they played each morning. Marisol would come to the toy room after breakfast to wind Pichi up. She had to keep her eyes closed until she felt the final click of her key. Then Marisol would spin her around and scramble out through the labyrinth of the play rooms, playing hide and seek. Pichi was always fastest when first wound up so it was fun for Marisol to see if she could outrun her and hide before she got caught.

Pichi sped through the rooms, on little wheels that she could pop out of the bottom of her feet like roller skates. It was easy for Marisol to tell where Pichi was because of the whirring of her skates and the clatter of things she carelessly knocked over in her wake. Marisol held back her giggles and crept on tip toes through the rooms managing to avoid Pichi at every turn. Sometimes when they played this game, Marisol would climb to the glass level and watch Pichi spin through the labyrinth for a long time, unable to find her. Pichi never liked it when Marisol played that way.

Marisol crawled on all fours through a tiny door in the

tea party room into the butterfly room. The butterfly room was filled with butterflies. There were monarchs and blue lilas and nymphflies and when Marisol entered the room they alighted on her arms and head and shoulders. That's when Pichi caught up with her, rolled too fast through the corridor and accidentally crashed right into Marisol.

Marisol fell over and Pichi landed on top of her. Butterflies scattered everywhere, filling the room with their rainbow colored wings.

"It's so beautiful," said Marisol, lying on her back looking up at the dancing wings.

"You're beautiful," replied Pichi, still lying on top of Marisol, staring at her pink heart-shaped lips.

FOUR

The first time that Pichi realized she was in love with Marisol was the time that Marisol told her about magic.

"Do you believe in magic?" asked Marisol.

"I don't know," said Pichi.

"I once met an old gypsy woman on the street in Oaxaca," said Marisol.

Marisol took a sugar cube out of her pocket.

"She told me if you write your wish on the sugar cube and put it in water it will come true."

Marisol handed a pencil to Pichi and instructed her to write on top of the sugar cube. Pichi had to write very small to fit the words on top of the cube. When she was done she handed the cube to Marisol who held it tightly between her fingers as she muttered some magical words. Then she dropped the cube into the cup of water and told Pichi to hold her hand over the cup.

When Pichi lifted her hand away from the cup after the sugar had dissolved, the words that she had written appeared in the palm of her hand: *I wish I was a real girl again.*

Marisol leaned over and saw the writing on Pichi's hand and gave her a hug. "You're still a real girl," Marisol whispered into her clockwork ear.

All the lights on Pichi's body glowed. She could feel Marisol's heart beating against the ticking gears in her own chest, Marisol's small breasts squishing against her own hard glass lightbulbs, the empty space between their flat bellies. Pichi knew that she would love Marisol forever.

FIVE

In the middle of the night, Pichi snuck out of the toy room and into Marisol's bedroom. She hadn't been out of the toy room since the first night she arrived and was worried that she really didn't know where Marisol's room was. The house was dark and the ceilings were high, the hallways seemed cavernous. In the dim light, she crept past each door and took care not to make any noise and she peeked inside each one, nervous that her squeaking joints would give her away.

The first room she found was filled with tropical birds. All the furniture was covered in feathers. The birds heard her open the door and stirred from their sleep. Some of them started to sing and a few of them flapped their wings loudly. She quickly closed the door and ran softly to the next door. It was locked. She kept going down a wrought iron spiral staircase and past a giant stuffed tiger whose eyes shone like it was alive.

When she finally discovered Marisol's room, the girl was asleep inside. Pichi crept to the edge of the bed and stared at the sleeping girl. Her face looked so gentle in her sleep. The toy girl reached out and rubbed her metal finger along the sleeping girl's arm. Pichi liked the way her skin was soft and flexible.

Then Marisol's eyes popped open.

"Pichi?" Marisol said rubbing her eyes.

"Hi."

"What are you doing out of the toy room?"

"I missed you."

Mariol sat up in her bed and stretched her arms out and yawned. "I missed you too," she said slowly through her yawn.

Pichi watched Marisol stare off into space for a few minutes looking like she was going to fall back asleep.

"So what do you want to do?" asked Marisol.

"I don't know."

"Want to play dragon?"

"What's that?"

"Climb under the covers, I'll get the flashlights. We pretend like we are fighting dragons."

"I don't need a flashlight. I have lights on my fingers."

The two girls played late into the night laughing and whispering. It was a happy secret, and no one ever found out about their rendezvous. Each night after that first time, Pichi would sneak out after midnight and Marisol would wait for her. Sometimes Marisol would fall asleep with her arms around Pichi, her dark hair tickling her metal skin and making her lights flicker.

It was hard for Pichi to leave the bed before the parents woke up in the morning, because the girl's warm sleeping body wrapped around her brass skin made her feel more alive. It was as if she could feel the blood pulsing through her own wires and gears, like they had merged into one creature. She wanted to stay that way forever but she knew that the mother wouldn't like it if she ever found out about Pichi sneaking out of the toy room.

SIX

"I know a game we can play," said Marisol's brother, Miguel.

"We don't want to play with you Miguel," said Marisol.

"But it's a lot of fun. I used to do it with all my tick-tocks," said Miguel.

"Okay, what is it?"

"You have to trust me okay?"

"Okay."

"First, you have to tie her up."

"Tie her up?"

"Yes, otherwise the game won't work."

"Is it okay if I tie you up?" Marisol asked Pichi.

Pichi was distracted. She hadn't heard anything that they had said because she was too busy admiring what Marisol had chosen to wear today. Her dress looked like it was made out of giant flower petals and it twirled as she walked. Marisol wrapped the rope around her hands tightening them in place.

Miguel stood behind Pichi and after Marisol had bound Pichi's arms he held her key in place so that it couldn't turn for a couple of seconds. When he released it, her body jerked around wildly.

Pichi was disoriented. She wasn't sure what they were doing.

"You're hurting her," said Marisol.

"She can't feel it," he said, "trust me, I've done this hundreds of times with tick-tocks."

"No. You have to stop."

Miguel grabbed Pichi's key to do it again, but Marisol slapped his hand away.

"Fine. Have it your way," Miguel said, "You never were any fun anyway."

"Come on Pichi, I'm sorry he is such a jerk," said Marisol taking Pichi by the hand. Pichi still wasn't sure what just happened to her.

SEVEN

One morning Marisol didn't come to the toy room after breakfast. Pichi waited. She climbed up to the second level and looked into every chamber in the toy room to make sure that Marisol wasn't hiding. Eventually, she couldn't search anymore because her clockwork had wound down so much she was running out of energy.

When Marisol finally showed up, Pichi glared, "Where were you?"

"What do you mean?"

"You didn't come at the normal time."

"What's the big deal? I come when I want to."

"But I need winding."

"I wound you up. You're fine."

Pichi wondered what was wrong with Marisol. She had never treated her that way before. She figured it was probably just her parents getting after her about something again.

EIGHT

The night of the full moon, Pichi and Marisol snuck outside in the middle of the night and went to the garden. They ran around naked under the stars. They climbed trees. Marisol bruised her knees and scraped her elbows. Pichi wasn't at all good at climbing, her mechanical body was not very agile.

"Did you see that?" Marisol asked.

"See what?"

"Fairies."

"I don't see anything . . ."

"Hello, Queen Mab, Queen of the Fairies," Marisol said to a rose. "We are honored that you are in our presence."

Pichi remained quiet. She wasn't sure who Marisol was talking to.

"Please visit us in our sleep and grant our wishes."

"But I don't sleep," said Pichi.

"Shhh, you'll scare her away," Marisol said and she gently held her hand palm up in front of the rose.

Pichi switched her lenses and leaned in closer, but still didn't see anything.

"Queen Mab wants us to dance for her," said Marisol, taking off her nightgown.

Marisol's skin was pale and gleamed in the light. Her dark hair fell past her waist covering her like a shawl. Pichi couldn't imagine there was anyone more beautiful than Marisol. Marisol did cartwheels down the garden path and started swinging her arms about, jumping over small plants and swinging from low tree branches. Then it started to rain. Marisol danced in the rain. Pichi stood there feeling the water seep through her brass skin and drip through her gears which ticked steadily. Marisol danced faster, her chest heaving in and out, a puff of her breath clouding the cool night air.

Marisol grabbed Pichi's hands and started to spin. She spun faster and faster until they both got dizzy, lost their footing and fell on the ground. Sitting on the ground it looked like only Pichi and Marisol were sitting still and everything else was still spinning around them. Pichi felt like they were the only two people in the world.

She saw Marisol's face turned toward the sky, her mouth open, rain drops bouncing off her teeth. And Pichi leaned over and kissed Marisol on the cheek. Marisol snapped her head to the side and stared straight into Pichi's bicycle wheel eyes. Pichi felt a tightness in her stomach. She thought she might throw up. She wasn't sure what Marisol's stare meant. She looked away, looked down at her hands. She suddenly felt naked even though she never wore any clothes.

"We should go back inside," Marisol said, her voice was flat and distant.

Pichi didn't say anything, she just stood up and offered Marisol her hand to help her stand up. Marisol pushed Pichi's hand aside and jumped to her feet.

"I'll race you there," she said, and grabbing her nightgown with one hand she took off running, her pale bottom glowing in the moonlight.

NINE

Pichi sat in the toy room waiting for Marisol to arrive. It felt like she had waited an eternity for Marisol. She was extra excited this morning because she had a surprise for Marisol.

While Marisol slept, Pichi came up with the idea to make Marisol a special toy. She collected bits of Maki's fur and some metal parts from toys that were never used and an old doll's body. She used glue and paint and created a little doll with a skull head and wings on its back. It had silver paint on its fingernails because that was Marisol's favorite color. On its chest was a little red glowing heart made out of a bottlecap that Pichi had found the night they went outside in the garden. In his hand he held a long sword made out of a ruler with a light attached to it.

When Marisol arrived, Pichi could hardly contain her excitement. After she was wound up she told Marisol to close her eyes and hold out her hands. Then she carefully placed the doll in her palms.

When Marisol opened her eyes, her mouth sprang open and she wrinkled her nose.

"Ew, what is this trash?" she said.

"I made a doll for you," Pichi said smiling. "He has a sword. He can help us slay dragons."

"Is this Maki's fur glued to his head?"

Pichi nodded her head proudly.

"That's gross!"

Pichi frowned.

"And what is this piece of metal? Is this from my toy train? You ruined my toy train? That was one of my favorite toys. You ruined it! You ruined everything!" Marisol threw the doll on the ground and ran out of the room.

Pichi stood there, looking down at the doll. It did look like trash. She wondered how she ever thought that Marisol would like it. She was sorry that she ruined everything. She wanted to cry but no tears came.

TEN

Pichi was distressed because Marisol hadn't come to the toy room yet. She could feel her clockwork gears slowing down. She knew that she didn't have much longer and she started to panic. She stepped through the door of the toy room into the sunlight in the hallway. She braced herself against the wall with one arm and slowly made her way down the hall. Maki followed her, then sprung in front of her. She was having a hard time balancing herself and was losing strength. She didn't need that springy dog under foot, so she shoved him aside with her heel and continued down the hall until she saw Marisol's brother.

"Miguel," Pichi called out, "Miguel, have you seen Marisol?"

"Nope, sure haven't," said Miguel.

"Please, you have to help me. I need winding."

"Not my problem. Find her yourself." He walked into the next room and slammed the door.

Pichi was starting to panic. She knew that if her clockwork stopped she would die. She had to find Marisol. She wandered frantically through the hallway. She wished that Maki was still with her so she could have his help finding Marisol. At last she reached the dining room. The table was covered in different sized platters all containing delicious meats and cheeses and piles of fresh fruit, but none of this interested Pichi, she just needed to have her key turned.

"What's this?" the mother yelled when she saw Pichi. "What are you doing out of the toy room? I don't need clockwork toys wandering the hallways while we have guests. Get back into the toy room this instant. Gregor, please, take this toy away."

"But. . ." Pichi tried to call out but she was too weak to speak and it just came out as a whisper.

Gregor picked her up by her clockwork wings, took her back down the hallway and threw her into the toy room. Pichi's gears rattled and she thought she felt something break.

An hour later, Marisol burst into the room laughing. She was arm in arm with a little blonde girl. They wore identical outfits and they were both laughing.

Marisol saw Pichi crumpled in the corner and came over to her and wound her up.

"What are you doing lying in the corner like that anyway?" she asked.

"You have a tick-tock, too?" said the blonde girl.

"Yeah, isn't she pretty?" said Marisol.

"Not as pretty as any of mine," the blonde girl said, crossing her arms in front of her chest. "I have four tick-tocks and they are all prettier than this one."

The blonde girl turned away from the doll. "But I'm getting too grown up for them. I was thinking of throwing them away."

Pichi saw Marisol's face and felt embarrassed. She wished she was prettier so that Marisol's friend would be impressed.

"You said you'd show me your costume collection," said the blonde girl.

"Oh yes, let's play dress up," said Marisol, leading the

other girl away from Pichi.

Pichi followed the girls to the costume room.

"Can I play too?"

"Tick-tocks don't wear clothes," Marisol said.

"This game is for real girls only," said the blonde girl.

Pichi didn't know what to say. She extended the wheels in her feet and rolled slowly backwards through the labyrinth into her little room. She sat there looking at walls that Marisol had helped her decorate. She had painted a mural on the walls with giant flowers and little fairies flying amongst them. There was a frog with three tongues and a giant eyeball creature named "Grog" that helped them on their dragon quests. Pichi pretended like she was playing dragon with Marisol. She imagined the story that she would tell the next time they were under the covers with their flashlights.

ELEVEN

Pichi knew just which stairs to avoid stepping on when sneaking out of the toy room at night so that she wouldn't make any noise on her way to Marisol's bedroom. They had not been playing together in the middle of the night for over a week now, and Pichi missed her company.

That night when she got to Marisol's room everything was different. All of the drawers to her bureau were open and all of their contents had been emptied out on the floor. Marisol sat in the center of the room with clothes and books piled around her. Her dark hair was wrapped up into a tall bun on top of her head and her brow was wrinkled in concentration.

Pichi wheeled over to her, carefully avoiding the messy piles. On top of the bed were four large luggage cases, lying open like empty coffins.

"I have a special adventure for us to play tonight," said Pichi.

"I can't play tonight," said Marisol.

"Why not?"

"Well, for starters, can't you see that I am busy?"

"What are you doing?"

"What does it look like I am doing? I am packing for school."

"So?"

"So? I'm too old to play games with dolls and I am leaving for school tomorrow."

"You're leaving?"

"Yes."

"For how long?"

"For a long time."

Pichi felt like her clockwork gears had been ripped out of her chest. She never considered that Marisol would ever leave. What did she mean that she was too old to play games with dolls? Pichi isn't a doll, she's a real girl, Marisol said so herself.

Pichi didn't know what to say so she got on her knees and reached out to hug Marisol. When she put her arms around her, Marisol's body felt rigid, like it was made out of wood. Pichi didn't feel herself tingling like she always used to when she put her arms around her before. Marisol's hair felt itchy and her pale skin made her look like a ghost.

Pichi let go of Marisol and the girl kept sorting her piles of things.

"Just go back to the toy room, will ya?" Marisol said.

TWELVE

Pichi sat at the window with Maki as the car drove Marisol away in the morning. Maki made a whining noise that Pichi had never heard him make before, and she nuzzled his furry gray head under her chin. She noticed that he needed winding and she wound him up. He sprang to life and danced around her as if he'd already forgotten that Marisol had left, or he at least didn't understand that she wouldn't be back.

Then Pichi started to panic. What would happen to her now that Marisol was gone? Who would come to wind her up each morning? Was she doomed to die? No, she wouldn't have that, she needed to figure something out.

She looked at Maki. She could wind him up and keep him going but could he wind her up? She looked at his patchwork fur and springy legs. There was no way. She would have to get someone else to wind her. None of the toys in the toy room would be able to help her. She would have to go to Miguel.

THIRTEEN

Pichi was afraid of Miguel. Nothing inside her felt good about asking for his help but she could think of no other option. When she went to Miguel's room she was nervous, she had never been in a boy's room before. It had a funny sweet fungal smell and everything was decorated in dark colors and it looked empty. When she walked into the room her foot passed through a red beam of light a few inches from the floor and an alarm went off. A computerized voice said "Intruder Alert, Intruder Alert" and then from a secret doorway behind a bookshelf Miguel emerged.

"What do you want?" Miguel said, pulling a book from one of the shelves and pressing a button hidden inside to shut off the alarm.

"I need you to wind me up," said Pichi.

"What will you do for me?" asked Miguel.

"What do you mean?" said Pichi.

"I will wind you up if you steal me three chocolate bars from the kitchen," said Miguel.

"Um. . ." said Pichi.

"Now," he said.

Pichi made her way to the kitchen. She was careful to avoid being seen. When she approached the pantry she heard strange noises coming from inside. She bent down and looked through a crack in the door.

"Stop making so much noise you naughty boy or I'm going to have to punish you," said a woman dressed in a short black dress and lacy white apron.

"I am a naughty boy," said Marisol's father.

The father stood naked with his back against the pantry shelves. The maid stuck an onion in his mouth and wrapped cheese cloth around his head to hold it in place. Then she pulled a wooden spoon out of the pocket in her apron and smacked his bare thighs.

"Mmmmmmm," the father mumbled through the onion gag.

"I have all sorts of ways to punish you today," said the maid.

She pulled an assortment of other items out of her apron pocket and held each one up to show him before setting it on the shelf next to her: a pair of tongs, a garlic press, a lemon zester, a mushroom brush and an ice pick. Pichi noticed that next to the ice pick was a stack of chocolate bars. How was she going to get the chocolate for Miguel? Pichi knew she couldn't go into the pantry.

Pichi turned around and searched through the cupboards near the pantry. She heard footsteps coming from the hallway. So she hid inside one of the cupboards, pulling the door closed, but leaving a little crack so she could see. The cook walked into the kitchen and pulled a big canister off the counter. She carefully measured flour into a bowl. She added sugar and an egg to another bowl and turned on the electric mixer. Then Pichi saw that on the counter behind the cook were two chocolate bars. She waited until the cook walked over to the refrigerator and Pichi popped out of the cupboard and wheeled across the kitchen grabbing the two chocolate bars from the counter on her way out the door back into the hallway. She squatted down to go faster and rolled all the way back to Miguel's room.

"Where's the other one?" Miguel asked as Pichi handed him the two chocolate bars.

"I. . .um . . ." said Pichi.

"I said *three* chocolate bars," said Miguel.

Pichi wasn't sure what to say.

"I'm going to have to punish you," said Miguel.

Pichi thought about the maid. Miguel burst out laughing.

"I'm just kidding," said Miguel, "You can make it up to me tomorrow."

Miguel wound Pichi up. He put his hand on her thigh and traced the grapevine lines etched into her skin. Pichi felt the lights on her hips flicker.

FOURTEEN

The next day Miguel asked Pichi to steal money from the mother's purse. She always kept her purse on her vanity in her bedroom.

"Are you sure I should do that?" Pichi asked. "I don't think it's a good idea stealing money from your mother. What if I get caught?"

"You owe me from yesterday," Miguel said. "Do it or I won't wind you up."

The mother's bedroom had a canopy bed with red silk draped from floor to ceiling. A wooden fan turned lazily above the bed causing the silk to billow slightly in the breeze. Giant white calla lilies grew from black pots. A large glass door led out onto a veranda. The door was open and bougainvillea flowers crept into the room on spindling vines. Next to the bed was the vanity.

Pichi wheeled along the tile floor and she grabbed the money out of the mother's purse and stuck it inside a pocket-like compartment in her stomach that she opened by pressing her belly button. After she put the money away, she looked at herself in the tall curved mirror attached to the vanity. She wished she looked more like Marisol. She wished she had rosy cheeks instead of shiny brass ones.

Pichi looked down at the makeup on the vanity. Marisol's mother had everything laid out in an organized way on top of a silver tray. She pulled the top off a tube of lipstick and applied it to her smooth metal lips. She

83

puckered her lips in the mirror and imagined what the lipstick would look like on Marisol. She wished that Marisol was there right now so they could put makeup on each other and play together. She had been so lonely since Marisol left.

Pichi lazily dropped the lipstick on the floor next to her and picked up the big goose feather powder puff. She dipped it into the cylindrical powder container and dabbed the puff against her face. The powder tickled the grapevine creases etched into her skin. As she removed the powder puff from her face she noticed a little circle of red on the feathers from touching her mouth.

"What are you doing you wicked doll?" the mother screamed at Pichi.

Pichi looked into the mirror and saw the mother coming up to her from behind. The mother snatched the powder puff out of Pichi's hands and accidentally stepped on the lipstick that was laying on the floor causing it to smear across the tile.

"How dare you touch my things. This is unacceptable," said the mother. She grabbed Pichi by the key in her back and dragged her out of the room. Pichi's feet scraped against the tiles, drawing a line of red lipstick from the vanity to the door. The mother tossed Pichi out the door and slammed it shut yelling, "Don't ever come in here again or I'll dismantle you."

As Pichi landed on the tile floor a piece of her knee broke off and clattered down the hallway. All the lights on her body lit up red in pain.

FIFTEEN

Pichi walked into Miguel's room, lipstick smeared across her lips and feet, her kneecap still missing.

"Oh Pichi, are you trying to look pretty for me?" said Miguel.

"I got your money," said Pichi in a low voice. She pressed her bellybutton to open up the compartment in her stomach. She reached in and Miguel said "Allow me," and he grabbed her wrist and pulled it away from her stomach.

Miguel stepped toward Pichi and pulled her wrist behind her body and held it against her lower back with one hand. With his other hand he reached into Pichi's stomach purse and slowly ran his fingertips along the inside lining.

"Kiss my neck," he said.

Pichi felt queasy. Miguel held her tightly and pulled the money from the purse, then he snapped it shut. Pichi kissed his neck and it left a red lipstick mark in the shape of a heart. Then he shoved her face first into his bed.

"This way my friends will think I've been with a girl," laughed Miguel as he wound her up.

SIXTEEN

Pichi sat in her room working on a new doll. She had taken more parts from the toy room and this time she was determined to make something worthy of Marisol. She took apart a Barbie doll and glued a picture of Marisol's face to its head. She dressed the doll in a miniature outfit she made out of Marisol's old clothes.

"Want to play dragon?" Pichi said to the doll.

"Oh yes, let's get Grog to help us," said Pichi in a higher pitched voice as she bounced the Marisol doll on her knee and looked up at the eyeball creature painted on her wall.

Pichi played dragon with her doll and looked forward to the day that she would be with the real Marisol again.

SEVENTEEN

Pichi came into Miguel's room. He had already turned off the alarm, because he was expecting her. He was sitting on his bed and told her to come sit beside him. He told her that she didn't have to do anything for him that day.

"Just sit still and let me look at you," Miguel said.

Pichi sat still.

Miguel wound her up very slowly. While he was winding her up, Miguel reached around and cupped her light bulb breasts. They glowed a very low light. Electric currents pulsed through Pichi's chest as Miguel gently rubbed his finger in a circle around her nipple.

Miguel reached his right hand down his pants and rubbed himself. He came around in front of Pichi, bent forward and licked her nipple. Little sparks passed between his tongue and her metal skin.

When he sat up he had his penis exposed.

"I want you to lick me now," he said.

Pichi shook her head no.

Miguel grabbed Pichi's hand and forced it onto his penis.

"Yes," said Miguel.

Pichi pulled her hand away from Miguel and ran out of the room.

"Come back here!" he yelled.

Pichi ran through the hall, knocking down a maid carrying a basket of laundry, and hid under a table in the toy room until she was absolutely sure Miguel wasn't going to come after her.

EIGHTEEN

Pichi played with Maki. They were playing fetch in the toy room and Pichi thought it was funny how Maki sprang all over the place, sometimes even bouncing off the glass ceiling.

"Maki, here doggie," said Pichi.

Maki bounded back through the labyrinth, carrying the Marisol doll delicately between his metal teeth.

"Good doggie," Pichi took the doll from him and replaced the face on the doll with another photo of Marisol wearing a different expression. Pichi had cut out pictures of Marisol and pasted them all over the walls to her room. She played with the doll and changed the photos in order to animate Marisol's expressions.

"Isn't it fun playing with Marisol?" Pichi asked Maki.

Pichi threw the doll and Maki ran after it. She knew she was kidding herself. The doll was no substitute for the real Marisol. Pichi looked up at the stars projected onto the ceiling. Maybe Marisol was somewhere looking at those same stars. Pichi thought those stars might bring them closer together like the night in the rain.

NINETEEN

The next day Pichi wasn't sure if she really wanted to go back to Miguel's room. The previous time had been really weird and she felt awkward and embarrassed. But the mother had threatened to dismantle her and the father was never around and the servant's weren't allowed to mess with the family's possessions unless ordered to. That left him as the only option.

"I've been waiting for you," Miguel said.

Pichi felt sick to her stomach. She approached the bed and Miguel already had his pants off. The skin around his scrotum was darker than anywhere else on his body and the tip of his penis was glowing bright red.

"I want you to suck it," Miguel said.

"I told you no," Pichi said.

"If you don't do it, I won't wind you up."

Pichi looked down at his penis, there was a tiny pearl of white liquid coming out of a hole in the tip. It looked like an eyeball crying a milky white tear.

Miguel said, "Come on, you can't last all day, you need me to wind you up so you're going to do it."

"No," said Pichi.

"You can't say no to me you bitch," said Miguel. He grabbed her arms and threw her down on his bed. He jumped on her back and shoved his penis against her. She struggled underneath him and he fumbled around trying to find an opening to jerk off with but Pichi's crotch was as smooth as a Barbie doll.

"What the fuck," Miguel said, bumping all around on top of her.

Pichi's lights glowed red.

"Ooo, you look sexier with those red lights," said Miguel.

Pichi squeezed her face in pain as Miguel flipped her over onto her back, still pinning her arms down. With his tongue he pressed Pichi's bellybutton and her little belly pocket popped open.

"Oh yeah," said Miguel as he slid his penis into Pichi's stomach. Miguel thrust in and out several times and then shuddered and fell on top of Pichi. She felt her stomach fill with slimy liquid and Miguel's penis went limp inside her.

Miguel rolled over and shoved Pichi off the bed. She looked up at him and said, "Aren't you going to wind me?"

Miguel ignored her.

Pichi tried to stand up but she was too weak. She crawled up to the edge of the bed and pulled on Miguel's arm.

"Miguel. . ."

"I'm not going to wind you."

"But I'm going to die. . ."

"You didn't do what I said," Miguel pulled his arm away from Pichi, "Get out."

"Miguel," she cried.

"Now."

Pichi crawled out of the room and back toward the toy room.

TWENTY

Pichi sat in the toy room barely able to move. She wanted to die, she couldn't go through this anymore, she didn't know when Marisol was going to return. Maki came springing into the room and dropped the Marisol doll in Pichi's lap. She saw Marisol's smiling face glued onto the doll and knew that she had to survive and find Marisol again.

She looked around the room and noticed a giant stuffed whale doll with a large open mouth big enough to climb inside. She crawled over to it and wiggled around until she felt the bottom of her clockwork key rest inside the whale's mouth. Then she let the weight of her body sink and she slid down to the ground until she felt the key turn slightly. She had to stand up straight again and reposition herself so that she could turn it a bit more.

It took Pichi all day and all night just to turn herself enough to give herself the strength to keep turning herself. She thought she would never be able to keep this up, but the threat of death kept her going even when she felt too exhausted to continue.

Maki sprung up from time to time when he needed winding and she took a break to help him out.

TWENTY-ONE

"Move those barrels right over there," came the mother's voice drifting into the toy room.

Pichi heard a loud rumbling noise and crept around the corner to see what was going on.

"I want all of this cleaned out in the next 24 hours," said the mother.

Pichi saw two men in blue jumpsuits and yellow hard hats standing at the edge of the room. One of them was wheeling a cart containing big blue barrels.

"Don't worry about sorting through any of it, I just want it all thrown away," said the mother.

Pichi popped the wheels out under her feet and rolled over to the mother.

"What's going on?" Pichi asked the mother.

The mother looked down her nose at Pichi.

"Oh, you're still around?" said the mother, "Well, Marisol is too old for toys, I am getting rid of them all."

"But what will happen to me?" asked Pichi.

"Good riddance, you were getting into too much trouble around here."

The mother hurried off and left the two construction workers there to clean things up. They worked all day, putting all of the toys into the barrels. Pichi saw the walls of her room knocked down as she was wheeled out inside one of the barrels. She saw the men chase down Maki and stuff him into a different barrel, but when they tried to put the lid on they found he was too big to fit completely inside. They cut his head off his spring neck, and tossed his head into a different barrel. Then a lid was put on top of Pichi and there was nothing more she could see.

TWENTY-TWO

Pichi didn't know how long she was in the barrel but it had been a bumpy ride. She knew she had to get out of there and find Marisol. After she kicked repeatedly, the barrel lid eventually popped off and she lifted herself out into the daylight only to see a vast landscape of twisted metal, tall weeds, and dirt. Corpses of rusted vintage cars formed cathedral like spires around mountains of junk.

Pichi ran over to the other blue barrels and pried them open one at a time. When she got to the last one, Maki's dismembered head was laying on top with his tongue hanging out.

"Maki!" Pichi cried out, cradling his head in her arms. She was alone. She gently put Maki's head back in the barrel and closed the lid like a tomb.

Pichi stepped carefully through the dirt trying to avoid sharp objects. She wandered down through the mountains of junk and came to a small grove of trees. Hanging from the tree branches were dozens of decapitated doll heads hung from rusted meat hooks. The heads looked like they'd been there for years, their hair matted to their heads from the rain and their cheeks caked with mud. The doll's glass eyes winked at Pichi as the heads swayed in the breeze. She started to feel afraid and lost.

Pichi climbed over piles of electronics, old TVs, and dismantled farm equipment. Her foot slipped on a cigar tube and she tumbled downhill wedging herself between a giant plastic Jesus figurine and a mountain of medicine bottles. Then she heard a noise above her.

"There's one," the voice called.

Out of nowhere, a crowd of clockwork toys came up over the mountain above Pichi and looked down at her. She scrambled to regain her footing and ran in the other direction. But she wasn't fast enough and the crowd caught up to her.

"Welcome to El Bario," said a tall skinny clockwork man.

"Please," Pichi said, adjusting her lenses to the harsh lights gleaming off their brass bodies. She stretched her arms out keeping the other toys at a safe distance. "What's going on?"

Pichi looked around at the faces. The tall skinny clockwork man had a face like a jack in the box, he wore a motley jester's hat and his torso was a giant spring. Next to him was a lithe ballerina standing permanently on one foot in a white tutu stained with rust and dirt. She looked like she had been beautiful once but the rouge had rubbed from her cheeks and her hair had been chopped off. Above her, hovering low in the air was a miniature clockwork plane and its tiny pilot wearing a leather hat and goggles called down to her in a high-pitched voice, "Hello," and waved a gloved hand above his head.

"We are the Noodles, we work for Dr. Garcia," said the tall skinny man, "My name is Jack."

"Who is Dr. Garcia?" asked Pichi.

"Dr. Garcia runs El Bario, he keeps us wound up and we help him find the others," said a big furry stuffed lamb in a sing-songy voice.

Pichi wonders if maybe these people can help her find

Marisol. She says, "Do you know Marisol?"

"Marisol?" said the ballerina.

Jack said, "No, but Dr. Garcia knows everyone. Come with us, we'll introduce you to him."

"Well, I have to find Marisol," said Pichi. "And, if I leave here, she won't be able to find me. All her things are here."

"Marisol was your owner?" asked Jack.

"Yes, she is the most beautiful girl in the world and . . ." Pichi stumbled, her clockwork was winding down and she couldn't stand up straight.

"Here, let us help you," Lamby sang as he leaned his thick curly fur against Pichi to prop her up.

Jack extended his spring torso and curved himself behind Pichi to wind her up. When she was all tightened, she sprang to her feet.

"Are there any more like you?" asked Jack.

"Like me?" asked Pichi.

"Tick-tocks," Jack said.

"I've never seen any others until today."

"That's what we do. We look for other tick-tocks and take them back to Dr. Garcia. Sometimes he is able to give us new bodies, synthetic bodies that don't have to be wound up."

"And you think he might know where Marisol is?" asked Pichi

"Well sure, if any of us need to know something we ask Dr. Garcia," said Jack.

Lamby nuzzled his head against her back, giving her a shove in the direction that Jack was leading. The tiny pilot buzzed around her head.

TWENTY-THREE

Pichi floated along the raft with the other toys down a river winding through the mountains of trash. Then they reached an archway that led to an underground city inside of the hollowed out mountains. Pichi lit up all the lights on her body to guide their way through the dark tunnels.

After a few moments, the arched ceiling started to open up and she could see buildings with lights in the windows. The buildings were constructed with adobe made from mud mixed together with bits of glass and doll limbs, car engines, sunglasses, pink flamingoes, old records and computer screens. Pichi saw other clockwork toys moving about behind the soda bottle windows of the buildings.

"Who are all these people?" asked Pichi.

Jack said, "We are all tick-tocks like you. We were all once human and were turned into toys and given as gifts to rich children. But all children grow out of their toys and this is where they are thrown. Dr. Garcia loves the toys. He helps all of us. He's a very good man and a smart scientist. He has figured out a way to transfer our brains into new bodies that don't require winding, so we can go back into the world and lead normal lives."

"Then why are you still clockwork?"

The jack in the box looks down at his hands, "It hasn't been perfected yet. It only works on one out of every three clockworks. But the rest of us have made a home here and we help Dr. Garcia rescue the other toys that have been thrown away."

"Maybe if I get a new body I can go to school with Marisol," said Pichi.

"Stop thinking about your owner," said Jack. "Don't you understand, she's gone, you've been thrown away. She might have loved you once but now you must start a new life and we're here to help you."

"You're wrong," said Pichi, feeling her gears tightening, she didn't like Jack's tone of voice, she wasn't sure if she really wanted to meet this Dr. Garcia or if these people were just getting in the way of her finding Marisol. If they weren't going to help her then she would have to find another way. But she knew that she wouldn't last long if she didn't have someone to wind her up. Her best chance was to try and get a new body. Then maybe Marisol would see her as a real girl and they could play dress up together and they would be happy together forever.

"Welcome home, Noodles," a voice said from the shadows. "What have you brought for me today?"

TWENTY-FOUR

Dr. Garcia wore skin-tight green spandex pants and a green sequin half-shirt. His hair was hot pink and stood straight up on his head like a feathered hat.

"Oh! What a beautiful creature you are," said Dr. Garcia as he ran his green-painted fingernails along Pichi's clockwork key.

Pichi sat in Dr. Garcia's workshop. There were gears and tools piled on long tables and a giant vat of blue bubbling liquid in the far corner.

"I hear you are looking for someone." Dr. Garcia put his hand on Pichi's shoulder and looked into her bicycle wheel eyes. Pichi saw herself reflected in his brown eyes. He looked at her tenderly, reminding her of Marisol.

"Do you know Marisol?" Pichi asked.

"Marisol. . ." Dr. Garcia rubbed his chin and wiggled his ears. "Nope. I don't think I do. Who is she?"

"She's my best friend," said Pichi, "and she left for school but I don't know where that is."

"I see," said Dr. Garcia. "Tell you what sweetie. I can't help you find your friend, but I might be able to release you from your clockwork prison. I can put you in a new body."

"Jack told me about it."

"Well, I have to warn you, it doesn't work 100% of the time. But if the procedure doesn't work, I want you to know that you will always have a home here with me."

"Okay, but I'm going to find Marisol either way." Pichi stuck out her chin and pushed out her chest pretending not to be nervous.

"We can get started right away, if you like," said the doctor.

Pichi nodded. "As soon as possible."

Dr. Garcia smiled at her. He took some measurements and had her stand on a scale. Pichi's metal parts clicked at him as he lifted her arms and examined her waistline.

"I'll need some time," he said. "But we'll begin soon enough."

Then he sent Pichi out of the workshop and told her to enjoy herself while he made the necessary preparations.

TWENTY-FIVE

Pichi was terrified about the surgery not working but told herself it would be worth trying because if she got a real body then Marisol would like her again and they could be together. She walked around in El Bario checking out the buildings.

She got lost among the winding streets of the underground junkyard town. Then she found an open pit filled with broken tick-tocks piled within it. It was like a toy graveyard. Dolls with no hair and crossed out eyes, lying legs akimbo criss-crossed on top of each other. There was a toy elephant that had been dissected, a mouse that was missing its arms and legs. And most disturbing of all, the remains of a clockwork girl very similar looking to Pichi with her belly pocket ripped out and clockwork gears spilling out of her eye sockets.

Pichi ran away from the pit and back through the winding streets, her gears ticking faster and faster until she came to a crowd of tick-tocks gathered together in a circle staring at something happening in the center.

Pichi approached the circle and peeked between the arms and legs of the people in front of her until she saw two clockwork men in the center wrestling each other. The men wore unitards and had bulging metal muscles. The lights on their body were lit up bright red and they circled around each other, slapping each other on the shoulder, each one trying to provoke the other.

Pichi noticed that the lights on the people crowded around the wrestlers were all blinking in unison.

"What's going on?" Pichi asked the girl standing next to her.

"A wrestling match," said the girl as if Pichi was completely clueless.

"Why are they fighting?" asked Pichi.

"For fun," said the girl.

Then Pichi noticed the smiles on the wrestlers' faces.

"They're wrestling toys, it is what they were designed to do."

Pichi watched as the clockwork men tackled each other. Whenever one of them landed a blow, a metal piece on the other man's body would flip over to reveal a fake bloody wound. The girl told Pichi their skin was double-sided metal on swiveling joints. When they got hit it didn't actually hurt them, it just looked gory.

TWENTY-SIX

Pichi went to the doctor's workshop the next day to have her surgery.

"Just try to relax," said Dr. Garcia.

Pichi's lights were flickering all over her body. Her gears felt like she was wound too tight, the wheels on her feet were spinning even though she wasn't standing on them.

"I'm going to slowly open your chest panel," said Dr. Garcia. "This shouldn't hurt, but let me know if you feel any pain."

The doctor unscrewed her ribcage and Pichi felt his fingers caressing the gears inside her chest. It didn't hurt but it made her feel funny. Then she felt a sharp pinch and she blacked out.

TWENTY-SEVEN

Pichi woke up for the first time. She looked down at her arms and instead of shiny brass they were fleshy pale skin, just like Marisol's. Pichi was more excited than she had ever felt.

"Oh good, you're awake," said Dr. Garcia. He walked over to her and put his hand on her forehead. "The surgery was a complete success."

Pichi smiled and reached her hand around her back and felt where she used to have her clockwork key. It was just smooth skin. She touched her head and felt hair, she pulled the hair in front of her eyes and saw that it was black just like Marisol's had been. She was happy.

"Would you like to see the new you?" asked Dr. Garcia.

"Yes," said Pichi.

Dr. Garcia wheeled a mirror in front of Pichi. She stood up, without thinking, her new legs working perfectly. She looked in the mirror and saw a woman, about 5'6, who looked to be about twenty years old, slender, long thick black hair, with black grapevine tattoos covering her pale skin where her etchings once appeared.

"What?" Pichi said. The woman's mouth in the mirror moving with her speech. "Wait, is that me?"

"Yes," said Dr. Garcia. "Don't you think you're beautiful?"

"What did you do to me?" cried Pichi. "This is horrible. I am not a woman, I am a little girl. Marisol will never like me now. She won't even recognize me. . ."

"Calm down," said Dr. Garcia. "You see, these bodies never age, so I could not have given you a girl's body. If I had then you would never grow up. You would be trapped as a girl forever. But this way you are already in a grown body and you will look young forever."

"But now I can never see Marisol again."

"You need to forget about her," said Dr. Garcia, "we will help set you up with a new life. You can be free to live your own life. You never have to worry about being wound up again."

"But, all I ever wanted was to be a real girl again so that Marisol and I could be together."

"You will forget about her in time," said Dr. Garcia.

"No, I won't forget about her. You don't know what kind of friendship we had. There will never be anyone like Marisol."

Then Pichi wiped at her face, trying to clean away the strange liquid that was leaking out of her eyes.

TWENTY-EIGHT

Pichi walked over to the gallery window. Painted on the window was a sign that said "Garcia's Gallery."

"Miss Garcia, could you please tell me about this piece over here," called an older woman. The woman was draped in a colorful shawl and had oversized gemstone rings on every finger. She stood next to a clockwork sculpture; it was a giant toy elephant with a tiny dismembered mouse running atop a spinning wheel inside its gutted clockwork body.

"That is one of my own creations," said Pichi walking over to the woman. "I take discarded toys and give them new life through my artwork." Pichi's tattooed skin was showing through the mesh fabric of her blouse. She wore a black pencil skirt and high-heeled shoes. Her fingernails were painted silver and her black hair was cropped in an asymmetrical bob.

"You have the most amazing things in your gallery," said the woman, "No wonder you are world famous for your clockwork shows."

A lot had happened to Pichi since she got her new body. She spent several years in El Bario helping discarded tick-tocks. But after a while she moved to the city and got her own apartment. She started showing her clockwork creations on the street, then at galleries, and eventually opened a gallery of her own. She blended in with society and even if they thought of her as an eccentric artist, most people that met her never learned of her past.

A young woman walked through the door. She had long black hair and brown eyes.

"Excuse me a moment," Pichi said to the bejeweled woman in the shawl. She walked over to the young woman, "May I help you?"

The woman stood admiring a life-size clockwork doll sculpture. It was hanging from the ceiling by invisible string so it looked like it was hovering in midair by two large wings made from wire mesh with ribbons woven through them in butterfly patterns. The butterfly wings fluttered as the doll was lit up from the inside with tiny flickering colored light bulbs. There were small wheels attached to its hands and feet. It wore a crown of roses on its head.

"I really admire this work," said the young woman, "I am looking for the person who runs this gallery."

"That would be me."

The young women clasped her hands in front of her chest and said with a huge smile, "I am so happy to meet you, I am here to talk to you about the apprenticeship."

"What is your name?" asked Pichi looking at the woman; she was wearing a form fitting dress with a deep plunging neck. Her skin the color of moonlight.

"Marisol Yvonne Reyes-Jimenez."

Pichi's breath caught in her chest. It felt like she was wound too tight. She hadn't heard that name in years. She looked at the young woman more closely and thought *could this be her, could this be my Marisol?* Pichi had tried to forget about Marisol, but not a day had gone by that she didn't think about her in some way. She wasn't sure how to react. Did Marisol come here looking for her?

"Have you been looking for me?" asked Pichi.

"Oh yes, I have admired your art for years. I am in grad school studying art history and the Garcia Gallery is world renowned."

Marisol's brown eyes held their gaze. She brushed a lock of her thick black hair out of her face and twirled it around her finger. Her heart shaped lips smiled.

"Miss Garcia," said the woman in the shawl, "Do you still have that painting you showed me last week?"

"Yes, the one with the three-tongued frog?" said Pichi, "I have it in the back." She leaned in and whispered to Marisol, "Excuse me one moment."

Pichi went into the back room. Grabbed the piece of art from the shelf and then froze behind the doorway when she heard the two women talking in the gallery.

"Miss Garcia is the master of reclaimed clockwork artwork," said the woman in the shawl.

"Yes, I know. Everyone knows of her," said Marisol.

"Rumor is that she used to *be* a tick-tock herself and that's why her artwork is so intimate," the old woman said. She twisted the lollipop-sized jewel on her ringed index finger and stared at Marisol. "So, are you going to be her new toy?"

"Excuse me?" said Marisol.

The old woman laughed, false teeth slipping inside her pink-lipstick mouth. "That's what we call all of Pichi's apprentices."

"Did you say Pichi?" asked Marisol. Her eyes widening as she turned her head to look for Miss Garcia.

"Yes, that's what her friends call her."

"Pichi…" Marisol said.

As Pichi stepped out from the back, carrying a painting

in her grapevine-tattooed arms, Marisol's mouth widened. Their eyes met as she stared at the gallery owner's face, which was becoming more familiar by the second. Even though Pichi's eyes were as human as hers, she imagined that they were spinning like bicycle wheels.

BEEHIVE GIRL

"…After that tango, we are no longer strangers…"

—Robert Heinlein, *The Number of the Beast*

ONE

Thick, golden honey drips from her beehive head which extends from her neck in a graceful oblong spiral, so tall she appears to be nearly seven feet in her purple stiletto heels. Her long muscular arms circle the shoulders of one of the old *milongueros* from Buenos Aires as he leads her across the maple wood dance floor. He is smooth and confident. He is dancing with the most desirable woman at the *milonga*: Maya, the beehive girl.

I've been consumed by the desire to dance with Maya since I started learning the tango. Her warm buttery honey scent, her glowing saffron eyes, the sinewy way she moves her hips, each movement filled with power and grace. She is bewitching. I've studied for two years dreaming of the day I would be good enough to dance with Maya. I am hoping today will be the day I get my chance.

Maya is my teacher's partner. Watching the two of them together is what turned me on to the dance. I saw them perform at a festival on the waterfront and fell instantly in love with the beehive girl. Her dress seductively revealed just enough of her honeycomb skin that I caught a glimpse of her inner thigh and the side of her breast as she moved.

After the performance, I went over to the couple, just so I could get a better look at her beehive head. She asked me, "What appeals to you most about tango?"

"Holding a beautiful woman in my arms," I replied, barely concealing the way my eyes undressed her body.

She smiled with a knowing look. I was embarrassed for a moment at my forwardness. But I could tell she admired my machismo. She appreciated a man who knew what he wanted.

"Then Carlos will teach you to dance," she said, squeezing her partner by the shoulder. That was the first and last time she ever spoke to me. Since then, she has never even noticed me at the *milonga*.

There were rumors that Carlos and Maya had a love affair. When I asked him about it, he denied it at first. But later he told me that, one time (and only once) after a particularly good dance, she forced him into her car in the parking lot and sucked his cock. It was the best blowjob that he's ever had, he said, the way the inside of her mouth vibrated sent him into instant, powerful climax.

I longed to feel Maya's embrace, if even for four short songs during one *tanda*. But she only dances with the best and most experienced men. If they make a single wrong step, it awakens her bees which emerge from the membranes on her skin and sting their faces and arms. Men have been known to get seriously injured from her stings. I've seen it happen more than once.

TWO

A woman seated next to me buckles her Comme il Faut shoes over her fishnet stockings. The stockings are too tight against her chubby skin which squishes out through the mesh in fleshy bubbles. She wears a dress that's just a little too tight for her. She must think it makes her look sexy.

I have danced with her before. Her name is Rachel. She has been a part of the dance community for years and is popular because she decorates the club for the milonga nights. But she's an unskillful dancer who has too big of an ego and thinks she's really hot shit. She likes to show off big fancy moves even though she doesn't have the skill to execute them gracefully. Some of the less experienced men are fooled into thinking she's amazing, but it's mostly because they don't know any better.

She rose through the tango scene really fast because she's always flirting with the visiting instructors from out of town to get them to dance with her. Sometimes she sleeps with them in exchange for private lessons.

I am not interested in dancing with her, so I try to ignore it when she looks over at me batting her false eyelashes. I have to be choosey with my partners. I know that if I don't dance with the best dancers, it will ruin my chances of attracting the attention of Maya. Like all seasoned dancers, she watches to see who the other women are choosing as partners, sizing up the men, waiting to see if they are worthy of her.

Rachel takes her glasses off and sets them in the center of the small table next to a round silver candle. Without them, her eyes look small and insecure but she never wears them while dancing.

"I heard that he's really good," says the blonde sitting next to her who is sipping a glass of *vino tinto*.

I pretend that I don't know she is talking about me.

"Who'd he study with?" the blonde asks.

"Carlos," says Rachel.

"The beehive girl's partner?"

"Yes. He's incredible. Though, I can't stand Maya."

"Why?" the blonde woman asks, placing her wine glass on the table.

"She always gets to dance with the best men. But how can they stand those disgusting bees?"

"I don't know. Do you think she has control over them?"

One of the bees flies over and lands on the rim of her wine glass.

"It seems that they only sting when she's pissed off," Rachel says, cracking half a smile. "I know I've had my moments of wanting to hurt the men who are terrible leaders."

"They are just attracted to her because she is young and smells like honey," says the blonde, flicking the bee off the rim of her glass with the edge of her fan.

I look over at the old man dancing with Maya. He is licking her neck. His wide flat tongue covered with sticky liquid, he laps hungrily at a spot under her ear. She only ever lets her favorite dancers do that. It's one of the most intimate gestures she allows. Carlos told me that she has to completely trust a person to let them taste her honey.

The old man squeezes the beehive girl tighter until

the open back of her orchid-colored dress is completely encircled by his arm. He gently cups her right breast with his fingertips. He raises his left arm higher in the air, cradling her hand with a scented handkerchief, so that she won't have to touch his sweaty palm.

Watching them, I want to be him.

I think the women next to me are just jealous. Neither one of them possesses the power of Maya. It isn't just her beehive skin or her honey. It's everything about her. She was actually considered kind of a freak when she first showed up in the scene. She came from Nijmegen. She studied at El Corte, the most popular tango salon in the Netherlands. Everyone had heard rumors about how brilliant a dancer she was, but when the other men first saw her, they were afraid of her. No one had ever seen a woman with beehive skin. But once they saw her dance with Carlos, she quickly became a favorite amongst all of the men. She was a challenge; she demanded the best of them. If they succeeded, it was like a badge of honor. If they failed, they were in jeopardy of serious pain. If they were ever stung, she considered it a disgrace and would refuse to dance with them again.

But the tango is a dance about pain, suffering, and longing. The idea that I would be putting my body at risk both excited and terrified me. I crave the sublime touch of her warm, waxy, vibrating skin at whatever the cost.

Carlos told me about a guy a few years back from out of town who thought that he was good enough to dance with Maya. He screwed up his *traspie* and ended up stepping on her toe. The bees swarmed from her skin, stinging him so badly he was hospitalized and later died of an allergic reaction to the bee stings.

Luckily, I am not allergic to bees, but that doesn't make me safe. The amount of stings her body could inflict would land anyone in the hospital. Which is why I have trained for hours, put hundreds of miles on the dance floor, and followed Carlos' every instruction and all of the traditional *codigos*. Finally, last week he told me he thought I was ready to ask Maya to dance.

THREE

Maya's set with the old guy is ending and I watch them glide around the dance floor like water on glass. She is the type of woman whom men would have held knife fights over in the old days. Her ass is a perfect apple shape, round and firm below her bee-sting waist. She leans against him *Apilado* style, her body and his forming an inverted V shape. Her strong legs, like two violins, in beautiful accompaniment with the longing pulse of the bandoneons and piano playing over the speakers.

As they pass me, spinning in a counter-clockwise direction within a large circle of dancers, a thick wave of honey-scented air warms my nose with orange, vanilla and clover flower. Herbal and soothing, it makes me ache to be next to her.

The bodies of the dancers are like knives, cutting time in slow motion, wrapping around each other like serpents and whips. They look like they came straight from the barrios of Buenos Aires.

My friend Patrick walks through the door, his dance shoes dangling from his left hand as he tips the coat check lady.

"Hijo de puta," he says in a bad Spanglish accent approaching my table. "Can you believe they raised the cover price again?"

He plops his ass into the chair next to me, accidentally shaking the table next to us, causing the blonde woman's glass of wine to spill over onto the white table cloth. She glares at him but he seems not to notice.

"I know," I say. "It's three times as much as last week."

"It's total bullshit that we have to pay more just because we're guys," he says, reaching down to pull off his street shoes and slip his feet into the handmade leather dance shoes.

The woman sitting next to us keeps looking over, giving him dirty looks. The blonde one turns her back to me.

"Can you believe these assholes don't think we're worth the cover price?" she says loudly, to make sure I can hear.

I ignore her. I do think its bullshit that guys have to pay more. We're the ones who have to spend hours training just to get good enough that a woman will accept a dance from us and then they make us pay extra just to have the privilege to ask them.

"Do you know if Carlos is coming tonight?" I ask Patrick.

"Dude, no. Didn't you hear?"

"What?"

"Last Friday he was hospitalized," Patrick says while tying his shoes.

"What? Why?"

"He dropped Maya during a *volcada*. It released her bees and he broke out in hives from the stings."

The blonde woman looks back over her shoulder. She's never one to pass up juicy gossip.

I lower my voice and lean over to Patrick. "Holy shit, but he was her favorite partner."

"Guess we all make mistakes, huh?"

"Is he gonna be okay?" I ask.

"Well, he'll never be able to dance with her again," says

Patrick. "Are you still planning to ask her tonight?"

"It's been my dream since I started learning tango. But now I'm even more nervous."

"Good luck, man."

"Thanks," I say, as Patrick catches the eye of a pretty brunette across the room. She winks at him and he stands up to greet her at the edge of the dance floor.

FOUR

The sound of a piano, like raindrops, falls from the speakers and bounces off the floor amidst leather soles of dancing shoes. A violin lets out a longing cry for its lost love as the next *tanda* begins. Since there are four songs in a tanda, I usually wait out the first song in a set to get a feeling for the orchestra and to decide who I should ask to dance for that music.

I look over at the DJ booth. The DJ tonight is Dan from Alaska. He's writing on a chalkboard sign that says *Now Playing*. It reads, "Gotan Project."

I remember Carlos telling me this was Maya's favorite music. They're a modern group from Paris whose sound is a mix of electronica and tango. I scan the room for her. She's seated at her usual table by the bar. I think this might be my chance.

Casually walking toward the bar, I keep my gaze softly focused on her table. I don't want to appear too eager, but I also want to make my presence known.

Maya sits with Graciela. Graciela is also from the Netherlands. Maya holds her honey hair off her neck and Graciela fans her with an ostrich feather fan while they converse in Dutch. She looks even more beautiful with her hair held up. The hexagonal patterns on her neck veined with bluish purple lines. Transparent wings of the bees stick out of the pores in her skin like soft peach fuzz. I long to press my cheek against hers.

She turns her head to face me. I look directly into her saffron eyes. I've practiced this many times before, the technique of asking for a dance using only your eyes. Carlos calls it the *cabaceo*. If she looks away, I'll know I've been rejected and no one else will have to know. If she maintains my gaze and smiles or nods her head then she has accepted my invitation. It's an old *codigo* of the dance and it has helped protect men's egos since the early days of tango in the immigrant brothels.

My muscles feel like they are ready to leap out of my body awaiting her response.

She maintains eye contact.

I can't believe it. The moment has finally arrived. Waves of nervous energy pulse through me. Buzzing, wild flower, hourglass feelings crawl just beneath the surface of my skin. She smiles and I nod my head. I wait at the edge of the dance floor as she stands, adjusts her orchid-colored dress and wipes a tiny drop of honey from her earlobe.

She steps toward the dance floor and I feel my heart start to race. My cheeks tingle, my palms itch, and I try to remember everything I've ever learned about how to dance well. I try to relax but I can barely breathe. She steps closer. I close my eyes halfway and prepare to take her in my arms, into the *abrazo*.

But instead of meeting me at the edge of the dance floor, she walks past me into the embrace of Dan from Alaska who is standing directly behind me.

Was she looking at him the whole time?

Damn these dim lights. Damn that skinny orange-haired bastard of a DJ who thinks he's so bad ass. I hate that guy. I have never been so mortified. I can't believe I thought it was finally my chance and it turned out that she wasn't looking at me at all.

I glance back at the table and see Graciela grinning at me. She saw the whole thing happen. She's laughing at me for thinking I was getting the chance to dance with Maya.

I don't even turn around. I hope that Maya didn't notice that I wasn't waiting for anyone other than her. I leave the edge of the dance floor and try to make it look as if I were just on my way to the bar all along.

I order a Grand Marnier. The scent of the syrupy orange liquid reminds me of the honey that drips from Maya's beehive head. I watch Dan caress her back and lead her in a perfect *cruzada*. That asshole moves like a truck. I can't believe he stole her from me.

They circle past me, the subtle buzzing of her bees is audible just under the nostalgic, soulful sound of the music. His style is forced. His movements, too big and flashy. He's more of a Nuevo dancer than the *Milonguero* style dancer she prefers, but she looks like she is enjoying it.

Patrick comes over and orders himself a Maker's Mark.

"Having a good night?" the bartender asks him.

"Yes, but it looks like my friend here could use another drink," he says, patting me on the shoulder.

"Make it a double," I say, holding out the empty brandy snifter.

"What happened?" Patrick asks.

"I got rejected by Maya."

I tell him the story about my failed *cabeceo*.

"That guy has a small dick," he says, motioning to Dan. I laugh.

"Seriously," Patrick says. "I saw it in the bathroom. Don't worry about him."

Patrick's humor is a little off, but I love how I can always count on him to cheer me up.

"Maybe Maya just didn't see you," Patrick says. "You should dance with Laurel. She'll make you look good. She always makes the guys look good. If Maya notices you dancing with Laurel, I'm sure she'll want to dance with you."

Maya and Dan circle the floor a third time. They stick to the outside edge of the *ronda*, like most experienced dancers do, so that they can be seen by the people seated at the tables surrounding the floor.

The outer edge dancers create the flow, maintaining equidistance between themselves and the other dancers, influencing the collective use of space. I learned rather quickly as a newbie, if I wasn't skilled enough to hold the line of dance and maintain the space around me and my partner, the old guys would force me with their elbows into the chaotic center of the *ronda* circle. When Maya gives me the chance, I will proudly dance the outer edge with her.

I continue watching them and almost find myself admiring Dan's moves, even though I still think he's an asshole. He must have learned from someone in San Francisco. I can see it in the placement of his feet, his noodle-like walk. He puts the beehive girl into a fast-moving *calesita*. She bends her knee, crossing it in front of her standing leg, forming the silhouette of a number four with her lower body as he tips her forward.

Light from the hand-blown glass chandelier flickers red and orange across her honeycomb skin. Each of her millions of hexagonal pores contains a bee, each tiny bee ass vibrating just beneath a thin membrane, causing her body to shimmer musically under the lights.

The bees start crawling up his arms and his hands are shaking. If he can remain calm, they might not sting him. But, he has tipped her too far off her axis. She falls forward and he has to step back to brace her before her weighted leg slides out from under her. It's too late.

The peach fuzz wings on her neck stretch out and bees fly up at Dan's face. Five of them slide their stingers through his lower lip as Maya catches her own balance.

"Boludo," she says in disgust; Argentinian slang for *idiot*.

She drops their embrace and struts off in the opposite direction of the room, leaving him at the end of the floor by the DJ booth. He clutches his hands over his mouth and reaches over the booth searching for a bottle of water. He finds one, but not before accidentally hitting one of the switches on the console.

The music abruptly changes from the orchestra to an old Morrissey song: *as I live and breathe, you have killed me.* Everyone looks over at him, surprised that their set was interrupted in the middle. But the lighting is too dim for them to see Dan's bee stings and they figure it must be one of his preprogrammed *curtinas*, the songs that are played in between the tango sets. It signals the dancers that it is time to change partners and everyone clears the floor.

I feel almost sad for Dan that he will never dance with Maya again. He will probably never DJ again, either. Word travels fast in the dance community. Once a guy screws up with Maya he's finished within a matter of days.

FIVE

The next tango begins. It is an Argentinian waltz. I go to the water fountain to get a drink while scoping out the room to see if Laurel is available.

I notice her by the DJ booth. I am about to walk nearer to see if I can make eye contact when Rachel corners me against the water fountain.

"Hi handsome," she says, licking her almond colored lips and stroking her hands against the bubbled flesh under her fish-netted thighs.

"Um, hi Rachel," I say.

"Have you seen Carlos?"

"Nope," I answer. I'm not sure if I should say anything about him being in the hospital. I don't know what she heard us say earlier and don't want to contribute toward ruining his reputation.

"Well, you *have* to dance with me," she says, flipping her hair over her shoulder. "I've been hearing the best things about you."

"I was thinking about sitting this one out," I say, trying to politely decline. "I don't really like waltz."

Rachel is the last person I want to dance with tonight.

"Oh, you can't not like *vals*," she says in a high pitched voice that scratches my ears. "Gustavo Naviera told me that *real milongueros* appreciate the enchanting beauty of the waltz."

"Who's Gustavo Naviera?" I ask.

"You don't know who Gustavo is?" Rachel said, raising her thin penciled-on eyebrows. "He's the biggest deal *Milonguero* in Buenos Aires. He appeared in that movie *The Tango Lesson*, with Sally Potter."

"Oh," I say, not really knowing or caring what she is talking about.

Maya steps onto the dance floor with another old *milonguero*.

"I partnered him when he visited Toronto for the tango festival last year," Rachel says, obstructing my view of Maya. Rachel loves to brag about all of the famous people she has danced with.

I don't know what to say in response. I can't turn down someone as well-liked within the community as Rachel without hurting my reputation. The women talk to each other. They are always trading notes about which men are the best to dance with. If a guy is rude or impolite to any of them, they all will shun him.

"It's just . . . my feet are hurting," I lie. "I think I'd better just sit down and rest them for a bit."

"Oh, so first it's because you don't like the *vals* and now it's your feet?" Rachel bats her false eyelashes obnoxiously. "I'm getting the impression that you don't want to dance with me."

She pulls her shoulders back, thrusting her cleavage in my direction.

"No, no, that's not it at all," I say, trying not to glance at her breasts. I wish she would just leave me alone.

Desperately, I glance around the room. Maybe I can make eye contact with someone and they will come and save me from Rachel. I don't see anyone. Even Laurel has started dancing with someone else.

"Well," Rachel says, tapping her foot.

"Um," I say while noticing her face turning into a scowl. There are only two songs left to the *tanda*. It would be a short dance. If we dance near Maya, I can show off what I have learned and she might notice me. "Okay. Let's dance."

We wait until the next song ends. Rachel practices circling her feet on the ground, pointing her toes, while holding onto the bar. I watch the guy Maya is dancing with carefully. It always impresses me how little movement those old guys make. It seems that the better you get at tango, the less you have to move.

"Let the woman do all the work," Carlos once told me. "That way you can dance all night."

I'm beginning to feel it as I get more experienced. Because the entire dance is improvised, I really have to focus and feel my partner to determine the next step. It seems like the more attention I put on getting in touch with my partner's body, the less I have to do.

Rachel and I step onto the dance floor and I focus on trying to connect with her. I take three deep breaths before initiating a single movement.

"What are you waiting for?" she asks. "The music has already started."

She doesn't realize no one else on the dance floor is moving yet either.

"It's a sign of respect to listen to the music for a few seconds before dancing to it," I say.

She shrugs her shoulders.

I hold her close to me and deeply inhale the scent of her hair: a mix of cigarette smoke and lemon Pine-Sol. It makes me cough.

She snaps her head back as I gently brush her hair out of my face. She frowns and pulls her hair over her shoulder. I recompose myself and hold my left arm out. She places her hand in mine, gripping it firmly. I shift all my weight to my right foot and we begin to dance.

Rachel sticks out her butt and arches her back, leaning her upper body at an awkward angle away from my torso. I shift my arm and lift up slightly on her rib cage to straighten her posture like Carlos has done to me so many times in practice. I want to make sure that we show good form.

Carlos told me that good dancers should know how to make any woman look beautiful even if she doesn't know how to dance.

"You're holding me too tight," she whispers in my ear.

I loosen my embrace, but only slightly. I navigate through the line of dance until I'm behind the old *milonguero* dancing with Maya. I am careful with my movements. I don't want to be too invasive. I want to show off just enough to get her attention.

"Did you see what Graciela is *wearing?*" Rachel whisper-yells in a catty tone over the music.

I try to ignore her, concentrating on the dance. I hope no one heard her. I would hate for anyone to hear my partner insulting Maya's best friend. It's already embarrassing enough being seen with her.

The old *milonguero* elbow-blocks me when I try to *ocho* around to get a better view of Maya and I fall back behind him. His squat round body barely allows him to see where he's headed over Maya's shoulder. But it doesn't matter. He is such a good dancer that he can feel every inch of space around them. His round belly acts like a gyroscope, guiding her movements, anchoring her balance. He spins in smooth, tight spiraling circles, like a merry-go-round. Above his grey fedora, her beehive head towers several feet. Her eyes are closed. She is dancing in his arms, fully absorbed in the moment, trusting him completely. Some of her bees dance on the brim of his hat, entranced.

The song ends and she opens her eyes. I wait for her to notice me, but her mind is somewhere else. She looks like she's waking from a beautiful dream.

"Osvaldo Zotto says you should lean forward more when leading me into the cross," Rachel says, pulling me toward her, gripping my shoulder with her left hand. Her breasts feel like two oranges stuffed in her bra. Hard and inflexible. I look down at the bulges beneath her blouse, I couldn't tell from their shape, but now that I've felt them pressed up against me, her tits are obviously synthetic. I hate fake boobs.

The voice of a lovesick sailor from the 1930's crackles out of the speakers as Dan plays an original vinyl recording from his classic tango collection for the next song.

"Um, okay," I say, figuring that Osvaldo Zotto must be some other famous dancer.

It's hard to relax when I feel like my partner is comparing me to all these celebrities. Doesn't she know how annoying it is? And I was not expecting her, of all people, to start giving me a tango lesson in the middle of our dance. She's so stuck up. I try to stay focused, maintain our position in the line of dance. But she starts wiggling her back side like a duck and flopping her leg around as if it's a sexy embellishment. I take a few more deep breaths and center my posture. *Focus on my parter*, I remind myself.

"And grip my arm more firmly," she says, squeezing

my hand in a vice-grip.

I want her to stop talking. I want her to just relax and feel my lead. I want to show Maya what I've got. I want Maya to look over at Rachel and wish she were the girl in my arms. If Rachel is talking while dancing, it means she isn't taking it seriously. If she isn't living in the moment, it means that I haven't done my job as a leader and transported her. I want Maya to see the same dreamy-eyed look on Rachel's face as the old guy was giving her. I know it's up to me to make this dance good. I have only one song left in this set to impress Maya.

But things just keep getting worse. Rachel makes really wide movements even when I lead small ones.

"You should practice being more creative with your lead," she says. "I know you studied with Carlos, so show me some of that passion. . ." She draws out the word *passion* as if blowing smoke from her mouth.

I bite my tongue. She is making no effort to follow what I'm leading. She has a mind of her own. The dance floor is crowded and I have to maneuver quickly to avoid collisions with other dancers. Her feet fly out in all directions. I can tell she is showing off fancy moves she's learned in a studio and doesn't care if it goes with the music or my lead.

"I practiced my embellishments with Luciana Valle," she says, pulling me into another couple. I have to literally hold her back from knocking people over. It's like trying to dance with a windmill.

I wish she would just stop thinking for herself and follow me. I know that Maya appreciates a simple, soulful dance filled with confidence and connection. Rachel is making our dance look like a cheap encounter in a pay-by-the-hour motel.

"I want to *gaucho* you," she whispers to me as if it were dirty talk. I feel the waxy texture of her lipstick against my earlobe as she says the words. Then she forces her thigh between mine, nearly tripping me.

I steady us and pull her into side step. She leans back into a dip, sliding her chubby fish-netted leg slowly up the inside of my pants.

It makes me feel sleazy.

I try to reconnect with her during a pause in the music and she high kicks backward. Her foot flies into the air and her spiked heel nearly nicks the back of Maya's partner's fedora. The old guy turns his head and gives me a stern look. A few of the bees nestling on his brim fly off and land on my collar.

Maya's eyes pop open. She's looking straight at me. Her bees crawl down my lapel and one of them slips between the buttons on my shirt.

Sweat drips off my brow. I try to stay calm like I've practiced. I know the bees won't hurt me if I remain confident and composed. But I'm terrified I might get stung before I even get the chance to dance with Maya.

"I used to take ballet," Rachel says, "I'm still pretty flexible." She draws her hand up my spine and squeezes the back of my neck.

Focus. I take a deep breath and slowly exhale. Maya is watching. Carlos told me I was ready, now I just needed her to see it.

"But you're so tense," Rachel says. She pulls on my left arm like she's using it to hold herself up. It feels like a ten ton weight. How can she be that heavy? I know I have to remain calm and keep my posture elegant. I rotate my shoulder slightly and adjust the way that I am holding her hand to mimic the posture of the old milonguero. Delicate, like holding a tea cup.

"That's better," Rachel says, massaging my neck, not even noticing the bees.

I keep breathing steadily and glide in tiny circular grapevine patterns. The basic and most elegant tango step. Forward cross, open step, backward cross, open step. Repeat. Impossible for Rachel to fuck up. More bees land on my lapel and I stand up even taller.

Maya is looking directly at me as the milonguero spins her around the floor. She licks a drop of honey from her lower lip.

I summon my courage and lead Rachel in my signature move. I've been perfecting it with Carlos for the past six months in the studio and I've been saving it until tonight to show Maya.

My signature move is a passionate *boleo*. I reverse direction midway through a pivot causing my partner's leg to wrap around both our bodies and snap back like a whip. It's a sensual and dramatic step.

The music winds through my ears. I continue spinning in grapevine spirals, bending my knees, lowering our center of gravity.

"I am finally starting to see why everyone was saying I should dance with you," says Rachel. It's the first nice thing she's said since we started. I think we might just be able to make it through this.

Sweat drips off my chin and onto Rachel's silicone cleavage as I hold her closer. One of her false eyelashes is peeling away from her face and sticking to my cheek. Her pulse quickens. Her stomach pushes out against mine with a sharp inhalation and she holds her breath.

My timing is perfect, the edges of the room start to soften and I feel the motion inside me ignite like a furnace. I start to lead the boleo, but Rachel's body stiffens.

Instead of following my lead, she seizes my shoulder and thrusts her foot back, whipping it in a semicircle behind her. Her spikey heeled dance shoe brushes past the ankle of the dancer next to us and catches on the hem of his partner's flouncy skirt.

Rachel's sharp stiletto tears a hole in the skirt and slices into the woman's leg, drawing a line of blood down her thigh. The dancer screams out in pain and clutches her partner. The music stops and everyone looks at us.

I can't react. My breath catches in my throat. I can't believe what just happened. I want to run and hide. I don't want Maya to see this.

But she's standing right next to us, staring, along with everyone else. Something tickles my chest hair. One of her bees is crawling under my shirt. I can't let it sting me. Please, no. I have to remain calm. I don't make a move.

Rachel looks around and when she sees everyone staring she lets go of me and says, "Why were they so close? Don't they know this floor is slippery? Someone must have put talc on this floor because my shoes are sliding all over it."

Without looking at us, the woman's partner whips out a handkerchief from his breast pocket and hands it to her. She places it against the cut on her thigh. She wipes away the blood and when she pulls the handkerchief away, it appears to only be a scratch.

"I don't have my glasses," says Rachel. "I can't see a thing."

The gentleman offers the woman his arm, escorting

her off the dance floor. As they walk away, the woman glares at me. No matter what the follower does in tango, it's always blamed on the leader.

"Sorry," I mouth to her.

She leans her head against her partner's neck and hobbles to a table.

The bee under my shirt crawls up my chest and onto my neck. Its tiny furry legs send chills up the back of my spine. I feel nauseous. The bees on my lapel crawl around in a circular pattern, staining my black suit with beeswax.

"What the fuck was that?" Rachel says to me, her voice a condescending pitch. "You should pay more attention to the space around you."

I stare at her incredulously. Is she seriously going to be mad at me for that? I didn't have anything to do with that crazy spasm of a move she made. I try not to react. Another one of the bees from my lapel crawls under my shirt.

"You completely embarrassed me," she says. "Don't ever ask me to dance again."

She turns and flips her hair over her shoulder. She stomps off, wiggling her fishnet patterned butt like a soccer ball.

SIX

I'm ruined. I'll never be able to show my face at this milonga again. All of my dreams of dancing with Maya are shattered. It will take me a long time to recover from that mistake. And after what she just witnessed, she may never give me another chance.

I go to the bar and order a last drink to drown my sorrows before taking off my shoes to go home. I wish I could talk to Patrick about it but he's hitting on a cute Asian girl in a green silk romper. She's stroking his forearm and staring into his eyes. I don't have the heart to interrupt him with my misery.

As I'm about to take a sip off my brandy snifter, one of Maya's bees flies off my lapel and lands on the rim of my glass. Then the bee on my neck crawls onto my earlobe. I consider brushing the bees off, but now it's the closest I'll ever come to having Maya touch me, so I let them stay. Plus, I'm afraid if I disturb them they'll sting me. Even though I know that I've already ruined my chances with Maya, I still don't want to be stung.

Then I see her. The beehive girl walks straight toward me. My knees feel weak. I can't look her in the eye.

I chug my brandy and move over to the hallway where I kneel down to untie my dance shoes.

My eyes follow her purple stilettos to the middle of the bar. I expect her to order a drink. The bartender looks at her and without speaking she turns toward me and places one foot in front of the other, angling her toes out slightly. Bending her ankles inward, she slowly caresses them against each other where they meet in the center of each step.

The bees on my skin start buzzing loudly. Her feet continue their hexagonal pattern toward me until they *click click click* onto the black and white checkered tile of the hallway.

"Don't take your dance shoes off," Maya says in her thick Dutch accent.

I look up at her statuesque body. From my kneeling position, she appears even taller than usual. Like a goddess. Like a Queen. Up close I see the smooth, translucent pupal bees in the pods of her skin. They glow like mother of pearl.

"You haven't asked me to dance yet," she says, looking down at me, smiling. A rivulet of honey drips from her head and falls in the space between us.

The tiny winged creatures on my ear and in my shirt fly up and snuggle under the straps of her orchid-colored dress. The ones on my lapel rejoin the ranks in her honeycomb hair.

The final *tanda* of the night begins to play. An entire set of La Cumparsita, the traditional last song of the *milonga*.

I'm confused. People usually save their favorite dancers for the last set. Why is she choosing me?

I straighten my spine and try to breathe. I brush my hair out of my eyes. My body trembles. I can't control it. They say in tango that your body cannot tell a lie. Whatever emotions you are feeling will come out through your movement. When you are holding someone in your arms, it's impossible to disguise how you truly feel. I have to get it together so she doesn't feel my nervousness.

I silently escort Maya to the dance floor. As we reach the outer edge, she steps in front of me, pressing her chest against mine. She feels like static electricity, warm peaches, sunny summer wildflowers. My breath quickens. The vibration under her skin sends a low rumbling pulse through my entire body.

I try to tell myself that it's just like I practiced with Carlos. I hear his voice in my head telling me to relax. I imagine my body opening, glowing with color, and allowing the energy to flow through my dance.

I step forward.

Damn. Wrong foot. She's on the other foot. Shit. Fuck. I am screwing this up already. Okay, stop thinking so much. Feel it.

Forward cross. Open step. Backward cross. Open step. I repeat it silently like a mantra.

I hold my breath.

I wobble.

My feet feel like someone coated my shoes in glue.

I have trouble pivoting.

The bees crawl around my lips, their feet warm and sticky. My hands shake like an addict.

"I love this song," she says, closing her eyes.

Maya slides her honeycomb arm around my shoulder and down my back, pulling me tighter against her. Her stomach expands and contracts with each breath.

I breathe with her.

Releasing my tension, I circle my arm more firmly against her. I straighten my posture and remember all of my training.

While beginning my next step, the song ends. I wasn't paying attention to the music. I freeze, mid-step. Maya gracefully extends her toe, turning her knee to brush my thigh. She vibrates the muscles on her abdomen, extending her movement to match the length of the last note.

"Did you hear what happened to Carlos?" Maya whispers in my ear.

A knot appears in my throat and I gulp. "Yes," I say, my voice comes out more timid-sounding than I intend.

A bee lands on my eyelid.

"You're doing very well," Maya says. "I like a simple dance."

Oh no. Does she think my dance is too simple? Is she just being kind? Is this what it feels like to be warned before getting stung? I need to step up my game.

"I like the way you handle my bees," she says.

The bee crawls from my eye to the bridge of my nose. I feel sweat drip down my neck.

I can do this, I tell myself.

I visualize the inner chambers of her honeycomb body. I center my balance and feel each individual muscle tense and relax along my spine. The next song begins.

I lower my left elbow and bring her arm in closer to my chest. We hold each other, listening to the drone of the bandoneon. It's okay, I tell myself, the first dance with someone new is always a little rocky.

I look down at her arm. Bees wriggle in and out of the holes on her flesh, doing their own version of the dance. They collect in groups, piling on top of one another. The ones on the bottom look like they are suffocating as more bees pile on top. A bee from across the room flies over to us carrying the carcass of another bee in its mandibles. It drops the dead bee onto Maya's shoulder and the dancing bees smash it into one of the wax filled chambers with their churning feet.

I steady myself and lean my torso forward, beginning my movement from my solar plexus as Carlos has taught me. I imagine a rod of light connecting our centers.

Maya responds to my lead and takes a step backward. Weightless, like an extension of myself. She inspires me. I listen to the hum of her body. We collaborate, synchronizing our expression of the music with each step; it's a conversation in movement.

Time drips slowly like honey from her skin. The melody of the tango transports us. Intensely focused; energy building within our bodies and then releasing into the circle.

She tilts her head, lengthening the side of her neck and says, "Would you like to lick me?"

I feel the pit of my stomach. All the moisture drains from my mouth. I look into her eyes and nod silently. Then I turn my attention to the side of her neck. Bees cluster around something under her ear. I am afraid to touch her with my lips. Afraid they will fly into my mouth. But instead the bees crawl to the sides and let me in, revealing an opening amid the blue lines on her honeycomb skin.

"You are so beautiful . . ." I say, leaning toward her. She presses her neck against my lips before I can say anymore.

Her wax coats my nose, almost suffocating. Crystalized granules of honey melt against the warmth of my tongue. Malty and sweet. The smell of baking oranges fills my nostrils. Her amber nectar slides down my throat, warming me from the inside.

I lift my head and tip her back, holding her firmly in my arms, planting my feet, balanced. Her skin is hot. The hole under her ear looks like an exotic flower. Delicate folds of skin layered around a small waxy bud. I lick the papery folds and they envelope my tongue, sucking me inside. I press my lips around the hard wax flower, sucking back, lapping at her honey.

The bees crawl from her neck to my ears, filling them with a vibration that matches the quiver of her honeycomb skin. I lose myself inside her. Slurping sticky liquid as it flows faster, thinning with our combined heat. Twirling my tongue between the folds of her skin until the hard bud completely dissolves like a piece of candy.

When the song ends, Maya says, "Would you be willing to replace Carlos as my partner?" Her saffron eyes, like the centers of sunflowers.

My heart feels like hot coals. I could die a thousand tiny deaths in this moment.

"Yes," I whisper, the 's' sound spreading across my face into the widest smile I have ever formed. I never want to leave her arms.

The music begins for a final time. Our bodies melt together. The warm orange-scented nectar glues us to each other. We share one heartbeat. I can no longer tell where one of us ends and the other begins. We are outside of time and space, looking in at a version of ourselves. The vibrations of the beehive girl shockwave through me like red spheres of light. Her purple stilettos whip around in perfect boleos. Each step a delicate balance of resistance and submission.

Her bees begin to crawl along my arms. They feel different this time. They are an extension of Maya's body, filled with her energy, joining us together. My vision shifts. Ultraviolet patterns reveal themselves on her skin like tattoos. They look like musical notation or advanced calculus.

One at a time, and then in groups, the bees dance from

her body to mine. Vibrating faster and swarming until they coat our entire bodies. We are completely enveloped by them. Every surface of our skin, between our legs, over our mouth and eyes, covered by millions of tiny bodies. Cocooned in bees, we move blindly around the ronda. Immersed in our own world, everything else drops away. Just music remains.

A humming vibration infuses my body. Subtle at first, and then strong like the pounding of a drum. It rises from the base of my spine, spiraling through my body like water through a seashell. Buzzing. Deafening.

I no longer know the difference between myself and the bees. My perception widens. I am every bee and every space in between them. I feel every molecule vibrating at the same frequency. My sense of self completely dissolves.

The last note of the last song falls upon the floor. And as the music ends, I become the bees. My thousands of wings beating like a symphony, hearing only the music of Maya's body. And as all else goes silent, I fly into the safe hexagonal compartments of her skin, through her honeycomb hair, deep inside her.

AUTHOR'S NOTES

Caterpillar Girl

As a teenager, I was obsessed with the music of The Cure. Posters of Robert Smith plastered my walls and I wore white face makeup and lots of black eyeliner. Following this band led to my discovery of tons of other weird cool shit and defined how I was categorized in High School. This story was inspired by two of my favorite songs, *The Caterpillar* and *Lullaby*. My first crush in High School was on another girl. She was also obsessed with The Cure and *The Caterpillar* was one of the first songs we ever made out to. I've always liked the idea of a caterpillar girl who changes into a butterfly, destroying the relationship that she's in. The song *Lullaby* is about a spider-man who sneaks into people's beds at night and eats them. I decided to combine the two concepts and make the spider-man a spider-girl.

Clockwork Girl

My writing mentor Carlton Mellick III inspired me to write this story which was originally published in *The Bizarro Starter Kit Purple* (Eraserhead Press, 2010). I based the plot around one of my most beloved childhood stories *The Velveteen Rabbit* by Margery Williams. When I was younger, I always imagined that my dolls were real people. I used to feel guilty for leaving them alone or neglecting them. There's nothing sadder than an unloved toy. I decided to tell this story from the point of view of a real girl who has been turned into a doll. I imagine this story set in Mexico. I grew up in the Southern California and I have a strong affinity for Mexican culture, the colors and flavors of Mexico.

Beehive Girl

When I visited my publisher Rose O'Keefe in Portland, Oregon, she took me to my first milonga—a place where people go to dance Argentine Tango. Rose is an incredible dancer, has been dancing tango for ten years and studied with the old *milongueros* in Buenos Aires. She taught me the customs or *codigos* of the dance and I was inspired to write a tango story. Around the same time, Bizarro super-fan Zoe Welch was turned on to my weird girl stories and suggested I write one titled Beehive Girl. Since honey bees communicate with each other through dance, I thought the two ideas fit together beautifully.

ABOUT THE AUTHOR

Athena Villaverde is a bizarro fiction writer from Toronto. She is a fan of kawii noir, fetish fashion, steampunk, Francesca Lia Block novels and Hayao Miyazaki films.

She is the author of two books: *Starfish Girl* and the forthcoming *Squid Girl.* Her short fiction has appeared in *The Bizarro Starter Kit (purple)* and *Demons: Encounters with the Devil and His Minions, Fallen Angels, and the Possessed* edited by John Skipp.

Visit her online at www.athenavillaverde.com

BIZARRO BOOKS

CATALOG   FALL 2011

ERASERHEAD PRESS

Your major resource for the bizarro fiction genre:

WWW.BIZARROCENTRAL.COM

Introduce yourselves to the bizarro fiction genre and all of its authors with the Bizarro Starter Kit series. Each volume features short novels and short stories by ten of the leading bizarro authors, designed to give you a perfect sampling of the genre for only $10.

BB-0X1
"The Bizarro Starter Kit" (Orange)
Featuring D. Harlan Wilson, Carlton Mellick III, Jeremy Robert Johnson, Kevin L Donihe, Gina Ranalli, Andre Duza, Vincent W. Sakowski, Steve Beard, John Edward Lawson, and Bruce Taylor. **236 pages $10**

BB-0X2
"The Bizarro Starter Kit" (Blue)
Featuring Ray Fracalossy, Jeremy C. Shipp, Jordan Krall, Mykle Hansen, Andersen Prunty, Eckhard Gerdes, Bradley Sands, Steve Aylett, Christian TeBordo, and Tony Rauch. **244 pages $10**

BB-0X2
"The Bizarro Starter Kit" (Purple)
Featuring Russell Edson, Athena Villaverde, David Agranoff, Matthew Revert, Andrew Goldfarb, Jeff Burk, Garrett Cook, Kris Saknussemm, Cody Goodfellow, and Cameron Pierce **264 pages $10**

BB-001 "The Kafka Effekt" D. Harlan Wilson — A collection of forty-four irreal short stories loosely written in the vein of Franz Kafka, with more than a pinch of William S. Burroughs sprinkled on top. **211 pages $14**

BB-002 "Satan Burger" Carlton Mellick III — The cult novel that put Carlton Mellick III on the map ... Six punks get jobs at a fast food restaurant owned by the devil in a city violently overpopulated by surreal alien cultures. **236 pages $14**

BB-003 "Some Things Are Better Left Unplugged" Vincent Sakwoski — Join The Man and his Nemesis, the obese tabby, for a nightmare roller coaster ride into this postmodern fantasy. **152 pages $10**

BB-004 "Shall We Gather At the Garden?" Kevin L Donihe — Donihe's Debut novel. Midgets take over the world, The Church of Lionel Richie vs. The Church of the Byrds, plant porn and more! **244 pages $14**

BB-005 "Razor Wire Pubic Hair" Carlton Mellick III — A genderless humandildo is purchased by a razor dominatrix and brought into her nightmarish world of bizarre sex and mutilation. **176 pages $11**

BB-006 "Stranger on the Loose" D. Harlan Wilson — The fiction of Wilson's 2nd collection is planted in the soil of normalcy, but what grows out of that soil is a dark, witty, otherworldly jungle... **228 pages $14**

BB-007 "The Baby Jesus Butt Plug" Carlton Mellick III — Using clones of the Baby Jesus for anal sex will be the hip sex fetish of the future. **92 pages $10**

BB-008 "Fishyfleshed" Carlton Mellick III — The world of the past is an illogical flatland lacking in dimension and color, a sick-scape of crispy squid people wandering the desert for no apparent reason. **260 pages $14**

BB-009 **"Dead Bitch Army" Andre Duza** — Step into a world filled with racist teenagers, cannibals, 100 warped Uncle Sams, automobiles with razor-sharp teeth, living graffiti, and a pissed-off zombie bitch out for revenge. **344 pages $16**

BB-010 **"The Menstruating Mall" Carlton Mellick III** — "The Breakfast Club meets Chopping Mall as directed by David Lynch." - Brian Keene **212 pages $12**

BB-011 **"Angel Dust Apocalypse" Jeremy Robert Johnson** — Meth-heads, man-made monsters, and murderous Neo-Nazis. "Seriously amazing short stories..." - Chuck Palahniuk, author of Fight Club **184 pages $11**

BB-012 **"Ocean of Lard" Kevin L Donihe / Carlton Mellick III** — A parody of those old Choose Your Own Adventure kid's books about some very odd pirates sailing on a sea made of animal fat. **176 pages $12**

BB-015 **"Foop!" Chris Genoa** — Strange happenings are going on at Dactyl, Inc, the world's first and only time travel tourism company.
"A surreal pie in the face!" - Christopher Moore **300 pages $14**

BB-020 **"Punk Land" Carlton Mellick III** — In the punk version of Heaven, the anarchist utopia is threatened by corporate fascism and only Goblin, Mortician's sperm, and a blue-mohawked female assassin named Shark Girl can stop them. **284 pages $15**

BB-027 **"Siren Promised" Jeremy Robert Johnson & Alan M Clark** — Nominated for the Bram Stoker Award. A potent mix of bad drugs, bad dreams, brutal bad guys, and surreal/incredible art by Alan M. Clark. **190 pages $13**

BB-031 **"Sea of the Patchwork Cats" Carlton Mellick III** — A quiet dreamlike tale set in the ashes of the human race. For Mellick enthusiasts who also adore The Twilight Zone. **112 pages $10**

BB-032 "Extinction Journals" Jeremy Robert Johnson — An uncanny voyage across a newly nuclear America where one man must confront the problems associated with loneliness, insane dieties, radiation, love, and an ever-evolving cockroach suit with a mind of its own. **104 pages $10**

BB-037 "The Haunted Vagina" Carlton Mellick III — It's difficult to love a woman whose vagina is a gateway to the world of the dead. **132 pages $10**

BB-043 "War Slut" Carlton Mellick III — Part "1984," part "Waiting for Godot," and part action horror video game adaptation of John Carpenter's "The Thing." **116 pages $10**

BB-047 "Sausagey Santa" Carlton Mellick III — A bizarro Christmas tale featuring Santa as a piratey mutant with a body made of sausages. 124 pages $10

BB-048 "Misadventures in a Thumbnail Universe" Vincent Sakowski — Dive deep into the surreal and satirical realms of neo-classical Blender Fiction, filled with television shoes and flesh-filled skies. **120 pages $10**

BB-053 "Ballad of a Slow Poisoner" Andrew Goldfarb — Millford Mutterwurst sat down on a Tuesday to take his afternoon tea, and made the unpleasant discovery that his elbows were becoming flatter. **128 pages $10**

BB-055 "Help! A Bear is Eating Me" Mykle Hansen — The bizarro, heartwarming, magical tale of poor planning, hubris and severe blood loss... **150 pages $11**

BB-056 "Piecemeal June" Jordan Krall — A man falls in love with a living sex doll, but with love comes danger when her creator comes after her with crab-squid assassins. **90 pages $9**

BB-058 **"The Overwhelming Urge" Andersen Prunty** — A collection of bizarro tales by Andersen Prunty. **150 pages $11**

BB-059 **"Adolf in Wonderland" Carlton Mellick III** — A dreamlike adventure that takes a young descendant of Adolf Hitler's design and sends him down the rabbit hole into a world of imperfection and disorder. **180 pages $11**

BB-061 **"Ultra Fuckers" Carlton Mellick III** — Absurdist suburban horror about a couple who enter an upper middle class gated community but can't find their way out. **108 pages $9**

BB-062 **"House of Houses" Kevin L. Donihe** — An odd man wants to marry his house. Unfortunately, all of the houses in the world collapse at the same time in the Great House Holocaust. Now he must travel to House Heaven to find his departed fiancee. **172 pages $11**

BB-064 **"Squid Pulp Blues" Jordan Krall** — In these three bizarro-noir novellas, the reader is thrown into a world of murderers, drugs made from squid parts, deformed gun-toting veterans, and a mischievous apocalyptic donkey. **204 pages $12**

BB-065 **"Jack and Mr. Grin" Andersen Prunty** — "When Mr. Grin calls you can hear a smile in his voice. Not a warm and friendly smile, but the kind that seizes your spine in fear. You don't need to pay your phone bill to hear it. That smile is in every line of Prunty's prose." - Tom Bradley. **208 pages $12**

BB-066 **"Cybernetrix" Carlton Mellick III** — What would you do if your normal everyday world was slowly mutating into the video game world from Tron? **212 pages $12**

BB-072 **"Zerostrata" Andersen Prunty** — Hansel Nothing lives in a tree house, suffers from memory loss, has a very eccentric family, and falls in love with a woman who runs naked through the woods every night. **144 pages $11**

BB-073 **"The Egg Man" Carlton Mellick III** — It is a world where humans reproduce like insects. Children are the property of corporations, and having an enormous ten-foot brain implanted into your skull is a grotesque sexual fetish. Mellick's industrial urban dystopia is one of his darkest and grittiest to date. **184 pages $11**

BB-074 **"Shark Hunting in Paradise Garden" Cameron Pierce** — A group of strange humanoid religious fanatics travel back in time to the Garden of Eden to discover it is invested with hundreds of giant flying maneating sharks. **150 pages $10**

BB-075 **"Apeshit" Carlton Mellick III** - Friday the 13th meets Visitor Q. Six hipster teens go to a cabin in the woods inhabited by a deformed killer. An incredibly fucked-up parody of B-horror movies with a bizarro slant. **192 pages $12**

BB-076 **"Fuckers of Everything on the Crazy Shitting Planet of the Vomit At mosphere" Mykle Hansen** - Three bizarro satires. Monster Cocks, Journey to the Center of Agnes Cuddlebottom, and Crazy Shitting Planet. **228 pages $12**

BB-077 **"The Kissing Bug" Daniel Scott Buck** — In the tradition of Roald Dahl, Tim Burton, and Edward Gorey, comes this bizarro anti-war children's story about a bohemian conenose kissing bug who falls in love with a human woman. **116 pages $10**

BB-078 **"MachoPoni" Lotus Rose** — It's My Little Pony... *Bizarro* style! A long time ago Poniworld was split in two. On one side of the Jagged Line is the Pastel Kingdom, a magical land of music, parties, and positivity. On the other side of the Jagged Line is Dark Kingdom inhabited by an army of undead ponies. **148 pages $11**

BB-079 **"The Faggiest Vampire" Carlton Mellick III** — A Roald Dahl-esque children's story about two faggy vampires who partake in a mustache competition to find out which one is truly the faggiest. **104 pages $10**

BB-080 **"Sky Tongues" Gina Ranalli** — The autobiography of Sky Tongues, the biracial hermaphrodite actress with tongues for fingers. Follow her strange life story as she rises from freak to fame. **204 pages $12**

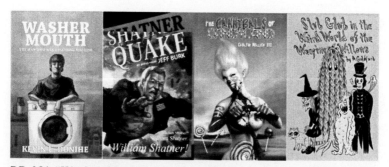

BB-081 "Washer Mouth" Kevin L. Donihe - A washing machine becomes human and pursues his dream of meeting his favorite soap opera star. **244 pages $11**

BB-082 "Shatnerquake" Jeff Burk - All of the characters ever played by William Shatner are suddenly sucked into our world. Their mission: hunt down and destroy the real William Shatner. **100 pages $10**

BB-083 "The Cannibals of Candyland" Carlton Mellick III - There exists a race of cannibals that are made of candy. They live in an underground world made out of candy. One man has dedicated his life to killing them all. **170 pages $11**

BB-084 "Slub Glub in the Weird World of the Weeping Willows"
Andrew Goldfarb - The charming tale of a blue glob named Slub Glub who helps the weeping willows whose tears are flooding the earth. There are also hyenas, ghosts, and a voodoo priest **100 pages $10**

BB-085 "Super Fetus" Adam Pepper - Try to abort this fetus and he'll kick your ass! **104 pages $10**

BB-086 "Fistful of Feet" Jordan Krall - A bizarro tribute to spaghetti westerns, featuring Cthulhu-worshipping Indians, a woman with four feet, a crazed gunman who is obsessed with sucking on candy, Syphilis-ridden mutants, sexually transmitted tattoos, and a house devoted to the freakiest fetishes. **228 pages $12**

BB-087 "Ass Goblins of Auschwitz" Cameron Pierce - It's Monty Python meets Nazi exploitation in a surreal nightmare as can only be imagined by Bizarro author Cameron Pierce. **104 pages $10**

BB-088 "Silent Weapons for Quiet Wars" Cody Goodfellow - "This is high-end psychological surrealist horror meets bottom-feeding low-life crime in a techno-thrilling science fiction world full of Lovecraft and magic..." -John Skipp **212 pages $12**

BB-089 "Warrior Wolf Women of the Wasteland" Carlton Mellick III
— Road Warrior Werewolves versus McDonaldland Mutants...post-apocalyptic fiction has never been quite like this. **316 pages $13**

BB-091 "Super Giant Monster Time" Jeff Burk — A tribute to choose your own adventures and Godzilla movies. Will you escape the giant monsters that are rampaging the fuck out of your city and shit? Or will you join the mob of alien-controlled punk rockers causing chaos in the streets? What happens next depends on you. **188 pages $12**

BB-092 "Perfect Union" Cody Goodfellow — "Cronenberg's THE FLY on a grand scale: human/insect gene-spliced body horror, where the human hive politics are as shocking as the gore." -John Skipp. **272 pages $13**

BB-093 "Sunset with a Beard" Carlton Mellick III — 14 stories of surreal science fiction. **200 pages $12**

BB-094 "My Fake War" Andersen Prunty — The absurd tale of an unlikely soldier forced to fight a war that, quite possibly, does not exist. It's Rambo meets Waiting for Godot in this subversive satire of American values and the scope of the human imagination. **128 pages $11**

BB-095 "Lost in Cat Brain Land" Cameron Pierce — Sad stories from a surreal world. A fascist mustache, the ghost of Franz Kafka, a desert inside a dead cat. Primordial entities mourn the death of their child. The desperate serve tea to mysterious creatures. A hopeless romantic falls in love with a pterodactyl. And much more. **152 pages $11**

BB-096 "The Kobold Wizard's Dildo of Enlightenment +2" Carlton Mellick III — A Dungeons and Dragons parody about a group of people who learn they are only made up characters in an AD&D campaign and must find a way to resist their nerdy teenaged players and retarded dungeon master in order to survive. 232 **pages $12**

BB-098 "A Hundred Horrible Sorrows of Ogner Stump" Andrew Goldfarb — Goldfarb's acclaimed comic series. A magical and weird journey into the horrors of everyday life. **164 pages $11**

BB-099 **"Pickled Apocalypse of Pancake Island" Cameron Pierce**—A demented fairy tale about a pickle, a pancake, and the apocalypse. **102 pages $8**

BB-100 **"Slag Attack" Andersen Prunty**— Slag Attack features four visceral, noir stories about the living, crawling apocalypse. A slag is what survivors are calling the slug-like maggots raining from the sky, burrowing inside people, and hollowing out their flesh and their sanity. **148 pages $11**

BB-101 **"Slaughterhouse High" Robert Devereaux**—A place where schools are built with secret passageways, rebellious teens get zippers installed in their mouths and genitals, and once a year, on that special night, one couple is slaughtered and the bits of their bodies are kept as souvenirs. **304 pages $13**

BB-102 **"The Emerald Burrito of Oz" John Skipp & Marc Levinthal** —OZ IS REAL! Magic is real! The gate is really in Kansas! And America is finally allowing Earth tourists to visit this weird-ass, mysterious land. But when Gene of Los Angeles heads off for summer vacation in the Emerald City, little does he know that a war is brewing...a war that could destroy both worlds. **280 pages $13**

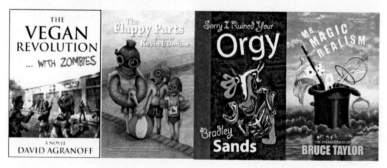

BB-103 **"The Vegan Revolution... with Zombies" David Agranoff** — When there's no more meat in hell, the vegans will walk the earth. **160 pages $11**

BB-104 **"The Flappy Parts" Kevin L Donihe**—Poems about bunnies, LSD, and police abuse. You know, things that matter. 132 **pages $11**

BB-105 **"Sorry I Ruined Your Orgy" Bradley Sands**—Bizarro humorist Bradley Sands returns with one of the strangest, most hilarious collections of the year. **130 pages $11**

BB-106 **"Mr. Magic Realism" Bruce Taylor**—Like Golden Age science fiction comics written by Freud, *Mr. Magic Realism* is a strange, insightful adventure that spans the furthest reaches of the galaxy, exploring the hidden caverns in the hearts and minds of men, women, aliens, and biomechanical cats. **152 pages $11**

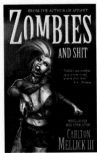

BB-107 "Zombies and Shit" Carlton Mellick III—"Battle Royale" meets "Return of the Living Dead." Mellick's bizarro tribute to the zombie genre. **308 pages $13**

BB-108 "The Cannibal's Guide to Ethical Living" Mykle Hansen— Over a five star French meal of fine wine, organic vegetables and human flesh, a lunatic delivers a witty, chilling, disturbingly sane argument in favor of eating the rich.. **184 pages $11**

BB-109 "Starfish Girl" Athena Villaverde—In a post-apocalyptic underwater dome society, a girl with a starfish growing from her head and an assassin with sea anenome hair are on the run from a gang of mutant fish men. **160 pages $11**

BB-110 "Lick Your Neighbor" Chris Genoa—Mutant ninjas, a talking whale, kung fu masters, maniacal pilgrims, and an alcoholic clown populate Chris Genoa's surreal, darkly comical and unnerving reimagining of the first Thanksgiving. **303 pages $13**

BB-111 "Night of the Assholes" Kevin L. Donihe—A plague of assholes is infecting the countryside. Normal everyday people are transforming into jerks, snobs, dicks, and douchebags. And they all have only one purpose: to make your life a living hell.. **192 pages $11**

BB-112 "Jimmy Plush, Teddy Bear Detective" Garrett Cook—Hardboiled cases of a private detective trapped within a teddy bear body. **180 pages $11**

BB-113 "The Deadheart Shelters" Forrest Armstrong—The hip hop lovechild of William Burroughs and Dali... **144 pages $11**

BB-114 "Eyeballs Growing All Over Me... Again" Tony Raugh— Absurd, surreal, playful, dream-like, whimsical, and a lot of fun to read. **144 pages $11**

BB-115 "Whargoul" Dave Brockie — From the killing grounds of Stalingrad to the death camps of the holocaust. From torture chambers in Iraq to race riots in the United States, the Whargoul was there, killing and raping. **244 pages $12**

BB-116 "By the Time We Leave Here, We'll Be Friends" J. David Osborne — A David Lynchian nightmare set in a Russian gulag, where its prisoners, guards, traitors, soldiers, lovers, and demons fight for survival and their own rapidly deteriorating humanity. **168 pages $11**

BB-117 "Christmas on Crack" edited by Carlton Mellick III — Perverted Christmas Tales for the whole family! . . . as long as every member of your family is over the age of 18. **168 pages $11**

BB-118 "Crab Town" Carlton Mellick III — Radiation fetishists, balloon people, mutant crabs, sail-bike road warriors, and a love affair between a woman and an H-Bomb. This is one mean asshole of a city. Welcome to Crab Town. **100 pages $8**

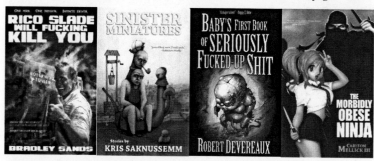

BB-119 "Rico Slade Will Fucking Kill You" Bradley Sands — Rico Slade is an action hero. Rico Slade can rip out a throat with his bare hands. Rico Slade's favorite food is the honey-roasted peanut. Rico Slade will fucking kill everyone. A novel. **122 pages $8**

BB-120 "Sinister Miniatures" Kris Saknussemm — The definitive collection of short fiction by Kris Saknussemm, confirming that he is one of the best, most daring writers of the weird to emerge in the twenty-first century. **180 pages $11**

BB-121 "Baby's First Book of Seriously Fucked up Shit" Robert Devereaux — Ten stories of the strange, the gross, and the just plain fucked up from one of the most original voices in horror. **176 pages $11**

BB-122 "The Morbidly Obese Ninja" Carlton Mellick III — These days, if you want to run a successful company . . . you're going to need a lot of ninjas. **92 pages $8**

BB-123 **"Abortion Arcade" Cameron Pierce** — An intoxicating blend of body horror and midnight movie madness, reminiscent of early David Lynch and the splatterpunks at their most sublime. **172 pages $11**

BB-124 **"Black Hole Blues" Patrick Wensink** — A hilarious double helix of country music and physics. **196 pages $11**

BB-125 **"Barbarian Beast Bitches of the Badlands" Carlton Mellick III** — Three prequels and sequels to *Warrior Wolf Women of the Wasteland*. **284 pages $13**

BB-126 **"The Traveling Dildo Salesman" Kevin L. Donihe** — A nightmare comedy about destiny, faith, and sex toys. Also featuring Donihe's most lurid and infamous short stories: *Milky Agitation, Two-Way Santa, The Helen Mower, Living Room Zombies,* and *Revenge of the Living Masturbation Rag.* **108 pages $8**

BB-127 **"Metamorphosis Blues" Bruce Taylor** — Enter a land of love beasts, intergalactic cowboys, and rock 'n roll. A land where Sears Catalogs are doorways to insanity and men keep mysterious black boxes. Welcome to the monstrous mind of Mr. Magic Realism. **136 pages $11**

BB-128 **"The Driver's Guide to Hitting Pedestrians" Andersen Prunty** — A pocket guide to the twenty-three most painful things in life, written by the most well-adjusted man in the universe. **108 pages $8**

BB-129 **"Island of the Super People" Kevin Shamel** — Four students and their anthropology professor journey to a remote island to study its indigenous population. But this is no ordinary native culture. They're super heroes and villains with flesh costumes and outlandish abilities like self-detonation, musical eyelashes, and microwave hands. **194 pages $11**

BB-130 **"Fantastic Orgy" Carlton Mellick III** — Shark Sex, mutant cats, and strange sexually transmitted diseases. Featuring the stories: *Candy-coated, Ear Cat, Fantastic Orgy, City Hobgoblins,* and *Porno in August.* **136 pages $9**

BB-131 **"Cripple Wolf" Jeff Burk** — Part man. Part wolf. 100% crippled. Also including *Punk Rock Nursing Home, Adrift with Space Badgers, Cook for Your Life, Just Another Day in the Park, Frosty and the Full Monty*, and *House of Cats.* **152 pages $10**

BB-132 **"I Knocked Up Satan's Daughter" Carlton Mellick III** — An adorable, violent, fantastical love story. A romantic comedy for the bizarro fiction reader. **152 pages $10**

BB-133 **"A Town Called Suckhole" David W. Barbee** — Far into the future, in the nuclear bowels of post-apocalyptic Dixie, there is a town. A town of derelict mobile homes, ancient junk, and mutant wildlife. A town of slack jawed rednecks who bask in the splendors of moonshine and mud boggin'. A town dedicated to the bloody and demented legacy of the Old South. A town called Suckhole. **144 pages $10**

BB-134 **"Cthulhu Comes to the Vampire Kingdom" Cameron Pierce** — What you'd get if H. P. Lovecraft wrote a Tim Burton animated film. **148 pages $11**

BB-135 **"I am Genghis Cum" Violet LeVoit** — From the savage Arctic tundra to post-partum mutations to your missing daughter's unmarked grave, join visionary madwoman Violet LeVoit in this non-stop eight-story onslaught of full-tilt Bizarro punk lit thrills. **124 pages $9**

BB-136 **"Haunt" Laura Lee Bahr** — A tripping-balls Los Angeles noir, where a mysterious dame drags you through a time-warping Bizarro hall of mirrors. **316 pages $13**

BB-137 **"Amazing Stories of the Flying Spaghetti Monster" edited by Cameron Pierce** — Like an all-spaghetti evening of Adult Swim, the Flying Spaghetti Monster will show you the many realms of His Noodly Appendage. Learn of those who worship him and the lives he touches in distant, mysterious ways. **228 pages $12**

BB-138 **"Wave of Mutilation" Douglas Lain** — A dream-pop exploration of modern architecture and the American identity, *Wave of Mutilation* is a Zen finger trap for the 21st century. **100 pages $8**

Lightning Source UK Ltd.
Milton Keynes UK
UKOW05f1031240614

233954UK00001B/20/P